Regret & Romance

A novel by Rebekah Santoro

Rebekah Santoro

Regret & Romance

ISBN 979-8-9876774-2-1 (paperback)
ISBN 979-8-9876774-3-8 (ebook)

Published by Oakwood Publishing LLC
www.RebekahSantoro.com

Rebekah Santoro

Dedicated to all those who were the right one at the wrong time.

Rebekah Santoro

Chapter 1: That Smile

Most people would prepare for starting their dream job by relaxing and getting a good night's sleep. Not me. Instead, I read a fantasy novel of considerable length well past the moon rising until I couldn't keep my eyes open, let alone feel anxious. Now I'm here, and golden sunbeams are shining bright on the old stone building standing tall and proud in front of me. Deep in my soul, I know it has to be the universe showing me the way forward and shouting, "Mel, this is it! Your dreams are finally coming true!"

I see my childhood self wandering through book stacks, as my much smaller hands run over the spines of adventures I had yet to embark on. A few short years later, I'm volunteering in high school to shelve on the weekends surrounded by that old book smell and friendly faces. Then, I'm pouring over my college textbooks late at night at the public library down the block from my university with my headphones blasting my best study music. Just in the last few weeks, I've made multiple trips to the library to explore the shelves in search of comfort and my next great read, even when I already have three books checked out on the Libby app on my phone.

Why was I even so nervous? This is exactly where I'm meant to be. I move my hands down the flowy skirt of my forest green dress before taking the dozen steps to the door of my new beginning at Erie Public Library.

"Hi Melody, we're so excited to have you join our team," my manager, Grace, says as she greets me inside the door of the library. She shakes my hand with a firm grip before gesturing for me to follow her into the staff room.

"Come with me and meet our other new employee."

I hear a voice. A voice that simultaneously makes my skin tingle and my stomach drop. Then I see his face. A few years ago, that smile would have made me melt. Now, it only brings me pain. The smile drops as his eyes meet mine.

Well, shit.

"Melody," is all he says.

What else could he say?

"James," I reply.

"It seems you two know each other," Grace says with an awkward smile.

I break my gaze from his deep brown eyes that have always reminded me of a pool of dark chocolate.

"We knew each other a long time ago," I force a fake smile on my face. "It's been so long, we're basically strangers."

I don't look at him to see how he reacts to my comment. I focus on Grace as she begins our orientation. *Pretend he's not here.* It's been almost five years. The last time I saw him, he practically *was* a stranger to me. I thought I knew him then, but I didn't. I definitely don't know him now.

Focus.

Duties at the circulation and information desks. Running programs each quarter. Assisting patrons on the computers. I have to concentrate on the present, not the past.

Flashes of a city covered in snow emerge from a hidden crevice in my mind. Moments that felt like eternity spent in a tiny dorm room run through my brain. The two of us exploring our college campus under starlight play like an old movie reel behind my eyes. I can still hear our twinkling laughter at a coffee shop where we spent many of our mornings together. My heart breaks in an old but familiar way.

Come back to the here and now Melody.

"James, as our new IT expert, you'll be floating throughout the library on technical needs as necessary, but the IT department is behind the circulation desk."

"Fantastic," he says as I keep my eyes glued on my new boss.

"So, how do you two know each other?"

Why couldn't she forget that bit of information? I swallow a groan and move my fingers through my hair, pulling my bangs back over the right side of my head.

"We actually dated in college," he answers before I have time to come up with something less telling.

"Of course, that won't cause any awkwardness or problems," I say with a confidence I don't actually possess. "We'll be nothing but professional."

My breathing becomes shallow, and I feel heat rising to my cheeks. This better not cost me my dream job. I've been desperate to get a foot in the door at a public library for so long. The jobs are scarce if you don't have a Master's in Library Science or if you want more than part time. Hell, they're scarce even if you are a genuine, certified librarian.

"Oh, I'm sure," Grace smiles, and the panic subsides a bit. "Melody, I'll have you shadowing Henry for the week as he prepares to embark on his new adventure in New York. We have another librarian who also works here, but he's on vacation and will be back next week. I'll give you both a tour, and then James, I'll be passing you along to our head of technology from our Main Branch, who will get you acquainted with all of our technical operations."

We follow Grace through the library, and as we trail her, she points out flyers of upcoming programs I don't hear the details of. Normally, I'd at least be appreciating the beautiful mahogany shelves filled with thousands of books, but I barely notice them. His presence so close to me is filling my whole body with anxious jitters, forcing my fingers to *tap tap tap* on the side of my thigh.

Grace pauses and points back to the staff room as she says, "I'll give you two a quick break, and then I'll introduce you to Henry and Maria."

Without sparing a second more, I beeline to the bathroom. When the door shuts behind me with a thud, I lean against it and take a deep breath; the oxygen pushing through me expands my lungs until they feel like they could burst. Then I release it. Once the exhale has fully left my body, I stand and move to the sink.

"This can't be happening," I say softly and stare at myself in the mirror.

The only thing I can do is attempt to distract myself with something other than the outrageous circumstances of my current reality. My light auburn hair is still in the waves I carefully set into place this morning thanks to an annoying amount of hairspray. My face, however, has taken on a sunken look and is paler than normal under the makeup I worked so hard on only a few hours ago. I even had my eyeshadow match my dress to make my hazel eyes pop, but now I realize there is a dusting of green that found its way under my eye making me appear ridiculous.

"Dammit, dammit, dammit," I mutter as I turn the water to freezing and run it over my hands until it's too cold for me to take. The cool water helps clear my brain and I'm able to pull myself back from a panic spiral.

"I think you're sending me some mixed signals, universe," I say quietly and interlock my fingers behind my neck, forcing my eyes on the ceiling as a slightly unhinged laugh escapes me.

James and I really are no better than strangers at this point. I can be professional. Right? There's no need to think about anything else. I have more important things to worry about. I can absolutely pretend he didn't shatter my heart into a million pieces five years ago with only a few words. Easy peasy, lemon squeezy.

I shake my head and cover my eyes with my hands.

Shit.

I take several more deep breaths before I'm convinced I'm composed enough to walk back out there.

"Can we talk a minute, Mel?" his voice says as I swing the bathroom door open.

Fuck me.

Well, not literally. Anymore. Goddammit. *Focus, Melody.*

"We have nothing to talk about, James."

I can tell by the way he flinches and then narrows his eyes that he fully expected me to call him Jamie, like he called me Mel. Like we used to. How could I though? Nothing is like it used to be.

"I don't think that's true." He opens his hands to me as a gesture of friendliness.

"Then you'd be wrong." I look away. "It's been almost five years, and I think we said everything we had to say in our last conversation. I'll be a friendly enough coworker, and I hope you'll be the same, and everything will be okay. Okay?"

"Of course," he throws his hands up in surrender.

A thought occurs to me I can't help blurting out. "How the hell did you even end up here? This is nowhere near Chicago."

"It's a long story." It's his turn to look away. He doesn't continue at first, but this time I wait for him to say more. "I started looking in the area for a job because I knew I needed a big change. I remembered how much you used to talk about growing up next to Lake Erie and how nice it was, and I couldn't think of anywhere better. I had no idea you were back in the area. I thought you were still in Chicago."

"How lucky for me." The sarcasm drips off my words. Oh, well.

I walk away without giving him the chance to respond. His steps follow behind me as I go straight to Grace at the information desk without another glance at him.

What I said is 100% true. I have nothing to say to him. Nothing that matters to the here and now, and that's all I care about. The past is the past. I *will not* let this affect me so much that I can't make it work here. He's somebody that I used to know, that's all.

Great, now that stupid song by Gotye is going to be stuck in my head for hours.

"All right, let's get back to it," Grace says when we are both standing in front of her.

He leaves to work with the head of technology from the main branch a few minutes later while I stay to train with the librarian that's leaving for New York. I'm grateful for the reprieve from Jamie's looming presence. I'm trying to be composed, but my thoughts and heart are racing. Agitation courses through me, making me want to tap my fingers over, and over, and over, and over. Memories appear in my mind each time I let my defenses down for half a second. How, in the ever living *fuck*, am I going to do this?

All I've ever wanted was a job in a library. My goal is to become a real librarian at some point, but until I get the money for that degree, I was hoping to get my foot in the door at a lower level. This may be my only real chance. But can I stay here when there's a constant reminder of the darkest days of my life lurking around every corner?

I have to. I can't risk going back to square one. Not when I just got my shit together. I can definitely ignore his beautiful light brown skin wrapped around those toned muscles and his bright white smile that makes my heart flutter. *Used* to make my heart flutter. Goddammit.

How the fuck does he still look like that? All that's changed is that he's gotten slightly older, bringing a level of maturity to his features I never thought I'd see. How do I compare? I've gained weight. I'm not overweight, but I've got more rolls than I care to admit, and these German birthing hips that have plagued me for years have only gotten thicker. Does he look at the older me and think about how much better I used to look?

It doesn't matter. I can't think about that.

I drag my attention back to Henry teaching me the circulation system, the layout of the different shelves, and where all the important areas are. There are so many resources the library offers, and I can only imagine the questions people might ask.

As the minutes turn into hours, I settle down and am comforted by how familiar it all is. I've spent my whole life in libraries. I may have only worked in my college library, but I've spent countless days browsing stacks and learning the ins and outs of how public libraries function on the other side as a visitor. Libraries are my passion. My escape. The place I've always been able to go to when the world is too big. Too overwhelming. I will not allow myself to be scared away by the stupid boy who broke my heart. I can't let him win again.

Yet, I can't help but watch Jamie as he moves through the library. His focus is on the other IT manager showing him around the space while my thoughts spin round and round about what working together will be like.

How many times have I wondered what it would be like to see him again? To have another conversation. Rehash how things ended. Maybe understand it all better now that we've grown and moved on. Have I moved on though? I'm sure he has.

"I've always loved the name Melody. Are you from a musical family?" Henry asks as he finishes showing a search in the catalog.

I take a second to pull myself back to the conversation Henry thinks has been two-sided when it's been more him talking and me nodding and 'uh-huh-ing.'

"Actually, I think it was more aspirational than anything else. My mom always said she wished she had learned how to play any instrument and thought maybe naming her daughter Melody would inspire me to be musical. I feel bad she was wrong because I don't have a musical bone in my body. Most of the time I just go by Mel."

"Well, Mel," Henry rubs his bald head, stands, and gestures to the rest of the library. "Erie Public Library is a great place to work. There're a lot of super nice patrons, and the entire staff cares about the work we do. I will warn you it's not uncommon to deal with tough people, but each day I go home feeling rewarded. As excited as I am to be moving to New York, this place will always be my home."

"I'm glad to hear you say that. I hope this is just the start of my library career."

Henry tells me about how his husband recently got a job as a principal in upstate New York, and he got in at a different but nearby school as the children's librarian.

"Childhood literacy is my genuine passion, so it was the perfect fit. And as much as I love the fall foliage in Ohio, I'm so excited to experience the leaves changing in New England."

He tells me all I need to know about being an Information Desk Associate. Hearing everything I need to learn about the job helps distract me from the elephant walking around the room. From checking books in and out to helping patrons browse the shelves in search of the perfect book, I can't imagine a job more perfect for me.

My biggest worry is I'll have to make suggestions for programs and events, and actually run them. I'll cross that bridge when I get there. Maybe it won't be so bad. I ignore the memory of me throwing up after my public speaking final in college. With it comes thoughts of being comforted by muscular arms and his soft words of encouragement.

Stop it, Mel.

Hours pass by swiftly as I absorb the information. Henry's a skilled teacher, and it's easy when you love what you're learning. Soon, it's the end of the day, and I'm exhausted and ready to be lying in bed cuddled up with my cat.

I glance around, but I don't see him anywhere. Hopefully, I can make my escape and pretend none of this happened. At least until tomorrow. I rush to the break room where I stored my things in a locker earlier this morning. Without bothering to put on my light jacket, I'm out the side door and hustling to my little red car.

"Mel, wait!"

You have got to be kidding me.

"Sorry, gotta go!" I shout backwards over my shoulder.

Even though we're about the same height, his legs move quicker than mine, and he's standing right outside my door before I can duck into the driver's seat.

"I just need one minute."

Rebekah Santoro

"Fine," I sigh and cross my arms. "What do you want, Jamie?"

"I know things didn't end very well with us, but I really want to be friends, Mel. When we were dating, we had so much fun together, and I honestly don't see why this has to be uncomfortable or weird. Especially since I know how much this job means to you."

"I don't think that's a good idea. We aren't friends. We're exes. It's been a long time since we've even spoken. I'm sure we're very different people now. We're coworkers. That's all we need to be. Let's not muddy the water."

His mouth is slightly apart, as though there are words trying to escape, but I keep my face emotionless and as firm as I can despite my stomach churning. His lips come together in a pucker. I fight the need to run my hands through my hair.

"Goodnight, James," I take a step forward so he's forced to move away from my door.

"I know I messed up back then."

I pause halfway in the car. Where the actual fuck did that come from? I have no idea how to even respond in a way that represents how those words truly make me feel. I stand back up and bore my eyes into his.

"That's nice for you, James. I knew that five years ago. It made little difference then. What does it matter now? Have a good night."

I plop down behind the wheel and slam the door shut. He's lucky I'm good at reversing. Otherwise, I might be a little too

18

tempted to swerve a little too far to the left and *accidentally* hit him with my car. I still hope I run over his toes as I speed out of the parking lot.

Damn. No dice.

Once I'm a few miles away, I call the only person who might make me feel any better about this nightmare of a situation.

"Holy shit, holy shit, holy shit, holy shit, holy shit," I spew when the phone connects.

"Uh-oh. This was not how I was expecting this call to begin," my best friend says when she answers, "It couldn't have possibly been that bad."

"Worse, Riley." I want to close my eyes and pound my head into the steering wheel, but I don't actually have a death wish.

"How?"

Cars rush by me as I obey the speed limit. I have zero interest in being a danger to anyone else on the road or, god forbid, getting pulled over.

"Another person just started today as well, and you'll never guess who it is," I say with a groan.

"You've got me. Spill," Riley answers.

"Jamie," I tell her in exasperation.

"Broke your heart in college, Jamie? Hurt you so bad you've never even told me, your bestest friend in the entire world, the details Jamie?

"That would be the one," the giggle that comes out of me is high pitched and breathless.

"Holy shit," she echoes my earlier sentiment.

"Exactly."

"What are even the chances of that?" She asks.

"I don't know." Out comes another anxiety induced giggle. "But whatever religion's God is the real one is definitely having a laugh up there."

"That's for damn sure. Do you want to come over?" her voice is already calming me down.

"I'm already on my way."

"I guess it's a good thing I stocked up on Moscato today," Riley says with a laugh, "And death by chocolate ice cream. Though I'm not sure those go great together."

"I'll be there in twenty. The wine definitely needs to come first."

"The corkscrew and glasses are already on the counter, and the door is open. See you in a few, Mel."

Chapter 2: Memory's Sweet Poison

"Okay, it's time you tell me everything that happened back then," Riley insists when we flop down on her gray couch, glasses filled to the brim with wine.

Where do I even begin? I tried to bury these memories so I could move past them. Not tuck them away so when I'm confronted with them in an unfortunate scenario of happenstance, I can recollect them perfectly. God. I want to scream.

I guess I'll start at the beginning.

Five Years Ago

I first saw his smile as a pair of elevator doors opened and thought to myself, "where has this smile been all my life?"

Though we had a class together and lived on the same floor in the dorm, our paths had yet to cross.

"It's Melody, right?" he greeted me in a smooth baritone.

"Yeah, but most people just call me Mel," I turned my gaze to the floor, embarrassed he knew my name, but I didn't know his.

"I'm Jamie," he saves me from my embarrassment.

I instantly yearned to touch him, so I offered my hand and said, "It's nice to meet you, Jamie."

His skin was soft and warm as he wrapped his long fingers around my palm. He shook my hand gently and let go; but I so wanted him to hold on.

"I didn't realize we live in the same building," he commented and moved to sit in a chair in the center of the room, motioning for me to join him.

"It's funny how that happens at a small school, right?" I grin at him.

His dark eyes found mine and shivers ran up my spine, so I found a distraction in the crowds of students walking outside the dorm. It was a little too easy to admire his toned body under his t-shirt and jeans. I wouldn't have minded getting that shirt off right then and there. At the time, though, my flirting skills sucked, so instead I asked about his major, as though our fields of study revealed deep truths about our souls.

"Computer science," he responded. "And you?"

"English," I told him.

"Ah, a bookworm," he grinned.

"Ah, a tech nerd," I tease back.

"I'm wounded." He put his hand on his pec and scoffed in mock offense. "I'm a tech geek. Thank you very much."

"Well, I am very much a bookworm," I laughed, "so you got me there."

"What's your favorite book?" he asked and leaned in toward me like he was actually interested in the answer.

"I don't know if I have one," I replied honestly.

"A bookworm without a favorite book?" his eyebrow arched.

"I think it depends on my mood," I shrugged. "There's just too many good books to pick one ultimate favorite."

"So what do you want to be when you grow up, Mel?" He leaned back in the chair and rested his head on the palm of his hand before blasting me with that perfect smile once again.

I immediately blushed and worried my answer would sound stupid.

"You first," I prompted.

"It sounds boring but I want to work in IT. Technology is easy to me and I like the idea of helping people make sense of it," he leaned forward again. "Your turn."

"I want to be a librarian," I thrust my chin out, defying him to make fun of me.

"That sounds like a perfect job for a bookworm," his eyes found mine again and I could tell he meant it with no judgment.

"I want to help people too," I continued on, "find books of course, but there's so many other great things about libraries too. Have you been to the one up the street? They just had a five million dollar renovation, and it's so beautiful. They've got movies you can check out, programs for everyone, computers for public use, even baking supplies, and so many other-"

I stopped myself from going on, certain he didn't want to hear me rant and rave about all the significant benefits of public libraries.

"Sorry, I don't mean to ramble." I turned my face to find anything but him to keep my eyes on.

"Don't be," he reached out to rest his hand on my knee and I looked over at him from under my eyelashes, "there's nothing better than listening to someone talk about what they're passionate about. Especially someone as pretty as you."

"Oh," my eyes found my hands, not entirely sure how to react, "thank you."

"It's my pleasure." He took his hand from my knee and I immediately missed the warmth of it on my leg. "Will you go on a date with me?"

I started in surprise, then stuttered a moment, before coming up with, "but you don't even know me."

"I've got a good feeling about you, Mel," he grinned while a burning fiery flame erupted in my core.

"Oh, do you now?" I leaned forward, mirroring his stance, "then a date sounds fantastic, Jamie."

I gestured for him to hand me his phone so I could enter my number. When I handed it back to him, the smile I was already beginning to crave turned on me.

As I walked away from him, all I could think was, "Did that actually happen? Where the hell did he come from?"

That's when everything changed.

On our first date, he whisked me away from campus under a soft evening sun and showed me his favorite place in Oakhaven. Under the bursting reds and oranges of the sunset, we walked through a park to reveal a hidden wooden bridge over a fairytale pond surrounded by trees.

One thought kept coming to mind the entire night; that smile was going to be the death of me.

"You actually grew up in Chicago?" I raised my eyebrows.

"Yeah, what's so surprising about that?" he wondered.

"Not surprising, just hard for me to picture. I grew up in a small town on Lake Erie. It's just so different."

"Well, I grew up in a slightly bigger town on Lake Michigan, so it's not too different," he laughed.

He pushed away from the edge and as his eyes began to drink up the colorful sky. I climbed up and sat on the rail.

"Stay right there," he demanded once I settled.

"Why?"

He pulled out his phone and pointed it at me before saying, "you're perfect."

"Oh stop," I blushed and turned my eyes to the sky. "Seriously, I always look terrible in photos."

"I definitely don't believe that." He walked over to me to show me the snapshot.

If I hadn't known any better, I wouldn't have even thought it was me. He had caught me as I was looking up at the moon shining bright, the sunset still behind me. My hands rested on my lap and I appeared utterly at peace.

"I think you just need someone who can appreciate how beautiful you are and capture it properly," he told me shamelessly. "Come on, let me take you to dinner."

Through the night, we learned about our lives before college, as well as all our hopes and dreams. He had a remarkable way of listening in a way I always felt understood, like he truly cared about each thing I said. When he spoke, I mostly thought I could listen to his smooth voice that reminded me of a cello playing a beautiful melody forever.

By the end of that date, we shared our first kiss, soon followed by our first night together. When our lips met, for the first time, I believed the movies might be right.

Lazing around in our dorm rooms missing a few pieces of clothing or going on adventures around Oakhaven and Chicago, Jamie and I became closer than I ever thought possible. We often went back to his favorite spot and talked for hours. Our connection in the bedroom, or dorm room, I suppose, was even stronger.

His touch was electric, always making me want to find a secluded spot to devour him. One night he took me dancing and despite the room being filled with people, our eyes were only for each other.

The one memory that will always stick in my mind was a night when we were walking around campus, stars glistening in the clear night sky, giving plenty of light. We found our way to a gazebo on the east side and he started playing "Something" by The Beatles on his phone. He laid his head on my lap as we sat on the wooden benches.

"Mel," he whispered in the dark and quiet night, "What is it about you that changed everything I thought I knew?"

"I keep asking myself the same thing, Jamie," I told him.

He took his hand and rested it on my cheek. I closed my eyes so I could focus on the feeling of his soft fingers. He stroked the side of my face once before leaning up and giving me the softest kiss imaginable as he ran his hand through my hair.

"I wish we could stay here, in this moment, forever," he whispered.

"We can make every moment as good as this one," I replied, my voice as quiet as his hand brushing across my skin.

"I'm not sure about that," he rested his forehead on mine. "Life never seems to work out the way I hope."

I wasn't sure how to respond. The talk of life was too big for me, so I went back to living in the moment, hoping it would never pass.

It always does, though.

While I floated blissfully on cloud nine with Jamie, I was unprepared for the darkness that would overshadow everything good.

My only three friends at the time, McKenna, Hope, and Carlos, stopped talking to me after McKenna decided she didn't want to be friends anymore. It was fine though, because I had Jamie. I was definitely fine.

Then there was Nicole. On our first date, I had noticed a message from her pop up on his phone, but I shrugged it off, figuring it was a friend or relative. Then I found out she was his ex-girlfriend and couldn't help but notice every time he turned his phone away to answer a message. Much too often, I wondered where he was when he wasn't with me.

But then we were together, our bodies and minds as close as possible, and I could think of nothing else. Every single word and glance made me fall in love with him before I knew what to do with myself. All of those bad feelings slithered away, and I forgot about them.

Until the next time I was alone. It all came thundering into my brain like a furious stampede of horses and I second guessed and questioned everything. I didn't want to face the truth. I was as certain as a person could be that he was falling in love with me as much as I was falling in love with him. Or at least that's what I told myself.

On the last day of school, my mom took the two of us out to dinner, giddy as can be to meet my first serious boyfriend. It was the calm before the storm because I had no idea what would come.

"Take a drive with me, Mel," he asked after we got back to my new apartment.

"Go, have fun," my mom winked and waved us away.

We drove around Oakhaven and he let me go on and on about everything and nothing for twenty minutes before finally interrupting with, "I think we need to take a break."

My face fell from a cheery grin to a frown of confused fear. What did he mean? Where did that come from? Everything was fine just a few minutes ago. Wasn't it?

"I don't understand," I said and began rubbing my leg.

"I realized this isn't what I need right now." He pulled into the gas station around the corner from my apartment and parked the car. "I'm sorry, but we need to break up."

My brain immediately pictured Nicole. This can't be because of her, can it?

"Is there someone else?" My voice broke, and I had to cover my mouth to keep from crying.

"No, I just-" he stopped and turned toward the window so I couldn't see his expression, "I need a break from this. From us. I I-still want us to be friends."

The fight left my body as I realized nothing I could say was going to make a difference. I didn't scream. I didn't beg for him to change his mind. One last look was all I had, and I wished I could see that smile one last time.

"Okay," I scoffed and shook my head. "I understand. Goodbye Jamie."

I left the car and walked around the block to my apartment thinking I only had to take a few more steps before I could break down. In my head I kept saying, "don't stop on the sidewalk and look like an insane person."

When I opened the door to my place, my mom had a huge grin that immediately disappeared when she saw my face.

I fell to the ground, my hands fisted and crossed over my chest as a sob overtook my entire body.

"Mel, what happened?" My mom rushed over and hugged me.

"He ended things," I got out after a few heaving cries.

"Oh, honey, I'm so sorry."

I think I cried on that floor for an hour before my mom forced me to get in bed where I could continue on with my heartbreak. Each moment replayed in my head. I parsed through every conversation, trying to figure out what went wrong. What did I do to make him not want me?

I lost Jamie. I lost my friends. Suddenly I went from having everything to having nothing, and my entire world shattered.

At first, I didn't even try to pick the pieces up. For the first month, I fell into a depressive hole that resulted in me barely eating and often doing things like crossing streets without looking. I tried reaching back out to my friends, but they wanted nothing to do with me.

I was a ghost of myself, and I didn't really care. Day after day, I went through the motions of being alive, all while feeling like I was too worthless to keep on living but was too much of a coward to do anything about it. I woke up and kept going. If only to hope eventually things would be better.

I thought I was doing good one day as I was working my summer job at the college library. Then, as I was cycling home, I pulled into my complex and saw Nicole going into an apartment. Then I saw him behind her, following her inside. I knew then there was always more than just friendship between them.

Shame and anger consumed me. I was mad at myself for being a naïve little girl who fell for someone that clearly felt nothing for me. The only way out was to grow to hate him instead of me.

Anger got me to the edge of that deep dark hole, kept me holding on to that edge and reaching for the light.

The sting of the memories faded, but they've always lived in my mind as a reminder to keep my heart protected. Or, because despite the last memory being one of pain, all the ones before that were beautiful and full of laughter and an almost love I couldn't quite let go of.

I couldn't let him go.

As I finish telling my story, my best friend is sitting on the couch crisscross applesauce, her chin resting on her fist. As she takes it all in, I think to myself that her dark red pixie cut always makes me wish I could pull off a cool look like that. Riley has five different pairs of glasses she switches between depending on the day and her mood. Today, she's got on the fifties style pointed corner ones that are black with a single diamond in the corner. She must be feeling vintage. Whenever she wears those, she talks about wanting to wear poodle skirts and drink milkshakes next to a jukebox.

I know Riley almost as well as I know myself, and I still didn't want to go through all this with her. It's so embarrassing and painful. I know she won't judge me, but saying it all out loud, I can't help but judge myself.

"So, he cheated on you?"

"I think so. Maybe physically, maybe not. It felt like every time he got a text I'd glance at his phone and see her name. He'd hang out with her and talk about her all the time, all the while assuring me it was friendly. But it doesn't matter because he broke up with me. Which is why I'm so embarrassed about it all! No matter the signs, no matter my gut, I was such an insecure little girl, and I let him destroy me. I was weak."

"Honey, that's a terrible way to think. Sure, you were young, but that doesn't mean you did anything wrong."

"If I had been smarter, I wouldn't have let this happen." I bury my head into a pillow before continuing. "I wish I had noticed the signs. He started pulling away. Started talking to Nicole more. The whole time I was thinking I must have done something wrong, or maybe he's not sure how he feels, but I didn't think a breakup was coming. I was so stupid. Here I was, practically in love with him, and he didn't even care about me."

"I'm sure that's not true."

"We only dated five months," I sigh, "but it felt so long then. It's humiliating to think about how strongly I felt about him in such a short time."

"That's the risk we take with love," Riley says. "You can be completely head over heels and the other person is only slightly interested. Sometimes, you don't know until you know. He shouldn't have been playing with you like that when he had his ex still hanging around though."

"I understand a lot more now than I did then. I thought I was completely over it, and then in one moment, it all came rushing back. Suddenly, all the time I spent convincing myself I was over it went up in smoke. Goddammit. The hurt is still there. I just buried it down deep and moved on with my life. I pretended until it was true."

"Fake it 'til you make it." Riley chuckles, "That's the best philosophy in life if you ask me."

I hide my face behind my hands because I'm afraid Riley will no longer see the confident, mature woman she declared she would be best friends with but the scarred and scared twenty-year-old that was an emotionally devastated idiot who let her heart get the better of her.

"What if you never make it?"

"The past is the past, Melody," Riley hugs me, and I'm so grateful for the steadiness of my best friend. "Don't let this turd-wagon take up any more room in your mind or heart. He's not worth it."

"Thank you, Riley," I squeeze her back as tightly as I can. "I have no idea what I'd do without you."

"Probably wither away from the lack of awesomeness in your life." She winks at me and gets up to refill our wine glasses.

We spend the rest of the night talking about less dramatic things and enjoying our favorite show, *Doctor Who*.

"I've decided we're going to be best friends," my memory recalls the day Riley announced our friendship was something I had no control over.

We had been working at the local Starbucks for a few months but hadn't really had the chance to interact too much. At first I was completely like, "What the fuck? Who says something like that?" Then it occurred to me. Why not? She seemed cooler than me, and friendly, and god knows it's difficult for me to make friends. Especially given what happened in college after Jamie. So, I decided to just go with it, and it was the best decision I could have made.

I was teetering on the edge of my depression when I met Riley. It was make it or break it on whether I was going to climb out or sink back to the bottom.

"Promise you won't ever stop being friends with me." A tear escapes and slides down my cheek, and she gives me another of her bear hugs.

"You're the best friend I've ever had. I could never!"

"Same," I smile and hug her back, grateful I'm no longer a lost and lonely little girl.

"I've just got to decide I will not let him get to me," I say to Riley, but I'm actually talking to myself. "Like you said, fake it 'til you make it."

"If that's how you're going to get through this, then abso-fucking-lutely." She turns on the next episode and chugs the last of her wine. "Whatever happens though, I'm here for you."

"You're the best."

"I know." She gives a winning smile, and we both settle back into the couch.

I spend the night at Riley's knowing I have a stash of extra clothes in her closet. There's been too many movie nights that have turned into one more glass of wine than we planned and we end up crashing at each other's places.

When I wake up in the morning, I lay quietly on Riley's couch, trying to calm my nerves. I focus on the birds chirping outside the window.

Think of the good things Melody. You got your dream job at a library. Riley is an amazing best friend. You have a settled and comfortable life. This is a bump in the road. One you can easily drive around and keep going. Or you can hit the bump head on, crash and fall off the road and back into the familiar hole you lived in for years.

I mentally flick the devil's advocate off my shoulder. I picture it as the twenty-year-old version of myself.

Riley still works at the Starbucks where we met but she has today off. On those days, she prefers her day to start much later in the morning than most adults. I'm showered, dressed, and out the door long before her eyes twitch open.

Anxiety causes my stomach to flip and rumble which makes me repetitively rub my thigh.

"I can do this. It's going to be fine."

I repeat these two phrases over and over to myself but I'm not sure I actually believe them.

The dread pools in my abdomen and turns into something resembling black sludge. The moment I turn into the parking lot, it turns to stone and sinks. He's standing outside his car waiting. For what? Who knows? It better not be me because I'm not giving his stupid beautiful face a second glance.

"Can we please talk, Melody?"

Why do these have to be the first words I hear today? I knew I should have stopped for coffee.

"I've said all there is to say James."

"I'm sure that's not true."

I turn and give him a glare before facing the building again and making my way inside. Stupid. Stupid. Stupid man. Please leave me alone.

"How's Nicole?" The question bursts from my lips without my brain's permission.

Why the hell did I say that?

"We haven't seen each other in a couple years," he mutters.

"I'd have thought you'd be married by now since you two just couldn't seem to quit each other," I bite out.

I sneak behind the circulation desk and say hello to Henry before Jamie can respond. Out of the corner of my eye, he slinks back to the IT office, his shoulders slightly hunched.

"Good morning Mel," Henry greets me with a wide smile and my frayed nerves calm a bit.

"Good morning Henry, it's good to see you."

"We're actually going to be at the information desk today, which is where you'll spend most of your time."

"Awesome," I smile at him.

I'm able to keep my attention on the work all morning and forget Jamie is even here.

"You're such a joy to be around Henry, it sucks you're leaving before I really get the chance to work with you."

"That's so sweet," he grins and I think a blush is creeping up his neck and into his cheeks. "If you're ever in upstate New York, definitely look me up."

At lunch time, I'm not as lucky as I was yesterday to be by myself. As soon as I sit down at a table in the staff room, an unwanted body plops down opposite me.

"Mind if I join you?" Jamie asks with a renewed expression of geniality.

"I do actually," I keep my eyes glued to the inked pages in front of me, "I have an awesome book I'm reading and it's finally getting to the good part."

"Oh, I'll be quiet as a mouse then," he smirks when I look up at him and I can only grimace.

As I'm getting to the part in my fantasy novel where the main character is discovering her magical powers, Jamie laughs at something on his phone and I'm pulled back into the real world.

"Sorry," he chuckles again. "You've got to look at this though."

Jamie tilts his phone so I can see the video of a cat stalking its owner and about to pounce. When it goes around the corner, the owner surprises it by pouncing first and the cat jumps almost three feet in the air, fur on its back standing straight, before landing and running away. A laugh escapes before I can stop myself and I immediately notice a satisfied look in Jamie's eyes which makes my grin turn into a scowl.

"Oh, come on," he says, "we can be friends Melody!"

I stay silent.

"I'm glad I found you two," Grace appears beside our table with a broad smile oozing excitement. "I have a special project I thought you'd both be perfect for!"

Oh, *come on.*

Chapter 3: Boys in Books are Better

"A special project?" I do my best to feign excitement but the prospect of working so closely with Jamie makes that impossible.

"The board and I had recently been discussing running a series of programs for seniors that teaches basic technology skills," Grace says. "Something of this scope would be best managed by two people and it'll get Melody acquainted with running a program. Jamie can be the IT guru on hand if any patrons have tougher questions."

"That sounds like such a great idea Grace," Jamie responds to her with a huge grin.

"Absolutely," I smile with my lips pressed tight together. "It's not a problem at all."

"Wonderful," she claps her hands together in front of her chest before continuing. "Our fall programs don't start for another month so I'll add it to the calendar by the end of today to begin the first week of September. Is that enough time to prepare?"

We both nod in affirmation, Jamie more enthusiastically than me. Grace leaves and Jamie turns to me with what seems to be his now usual smirk.

"I'll repeat myself since you can't seem to grasp the concept; we're just coworkers," I say as firmly as I can. "It's inevitable we'd have to work together on something."

I shrug as casually as I can when my instincts are telling me to curl up in a ball and pretend the rest of the world doesn't exist. I picture little versions of myself at a control table inside my head like the emotions from the movie, *Inside Out*, and they're all screaming and running around the room bumping into each other while the panel goes haywire.

"If you'll excuse me," I stand tall and march my way out of the lunchroom.

Once I'm through the door and I'm sure no one can see me, I lean against the wall and scrunch down to the floor.

UGHHHHHHHHHHHHHHHHHHHHHHH

The text I send to Riley goes through quickly and I thank goodness her response is even quicker.

Whatever happened, you're gonna be okay. You're a strong, badass woman and you can take on anything if you just believe in yourself.

I read the text over and over as a mantra and hope she's right and not saying things to make me feel better. Although, I suppose both could be true. After thirty seconds of wallowing, I stand up and get back to work, ignoring Jamie completely when he walks by the information desk.

"Hi, I was wondering if you could help me find a book?" a deep voice pulls me from my internal dialogue of anxiety conversations with myself.

I peel my eyes from the computer screen and am surprised by the handsome face in front of me. I immediately sit up straighter and give him my best smile.

"Absolutely, I can," I turn to the cataloging system. "What's the title of the book?"

"See, that's the issue," he gives a half smile along with an 'I'm ashamed I don't know' shrug. "I know it's a fantasy by a pretty popular author, but I can't remember the title. It's about a princess trying to save her home from religious fanatics and an exiled prince."

"I don't even have to look it up," I tell him with a dopey grin, "I know exactly what you're looking for. It's called *Elantris* by Brandon Sanderson."

"That's it!" He claps and leans forward with his arms on the desk. "How did you know that off the top of your head?"

"Fantasy is my specialty," I try to sound more cool and less nerdy but I'm pretty sure it doesn't come across that way.

"I've always been more of a sci-fi guy myself but lately I've been dipping my toes into the fantasy world and loving it. My name is Sebastian by the way. I haven't seen you here before."

"I'm new," I stand up and shake his hand because I have no sense of how to flirt and can only manage cute professionalism. "I'm Melody."

"It's nice to meet you Melody," he shakes my hand back and we both smile at each other before he tells me about how he recently read the first *Lord of the Rings* book and loved it.

As we discuss a book I've read enough times to know parts of it by heart, I fantasize Sebastian is a warrior from Celtic myth with his scarlet hair and tall, broad stature, jumping through time to find his lost love who just happens to be me in a past life. God, I read too much.

"Anyway, I definitely plan on reading the complete series plus *The Hobbit.*"

"You definitely should, it's a staple of the genre," I try to pull my best flirty face, inspired by Riley, and continue with, "if you ever need any more help or recommendations, let me know."

"Oh I will," he grins and I give a giggle in response before mentally smacking myself for acting like a stupid little teenager even as I wave to him walking away.

An unexpected voice from behind my shoulder makes me jump, "I don't like that guy."

"You didn't even talk to him," I turn to Jamie and give him my best scowl. "And I'm certain you don't know him and therefore can't have an opinion like that."

"I get a weird vibe from him," he furrows his brow as he stares the back of him down.

"Well, excuse me if I put little stock in your opinions James," I coat my words with iciness while narrowing my eyes.

Jamie's lips move apart almost imperceptibly and his eyes narrow in return, like he wants to snap back, but he holds it in.

"All right, I've got the series added to the calendar!" Grace struts up beside us and clearly senses the tension because she then asks, "Am I interrupting something?"

"Oh, we were discussing the best way to run the program," I lie. "We had a slight disagreement on whether we should start off with accessing email or using a search engine."

"Ooh good question," she looks up to the ceiling as if that would give her the right answer, "I would think probably using a search engine first but truthfully it may not matter. Maybe you can look up examples of other libraries' programs."

"What a good point. I'll go do that right now."

I turn away from them both and get to work. Even though I'm focused on the task at hand, my brain always finds a way to wander. At first, I'm thinking about Sebastian's wavy red hair and strong arms. I'm definitely not thinking about how good Jamie looks today in his tight button up navy shirt with the sleeves rolled up to his elbows and dark khaki pants. Not at all.

For a while, Jamie goes back to his office behind the circulation desk and I can pay attention to assisting patrons. I help two people find books they were dying to read as well as an older man find a movie he hadn't seen in thirty years he's been itching to watch again. The next person I assist is a teenager who can't figure out how to copy posters they're making for their French club at school.

"Do you have anything about the language of flowers?" Asks a middle aged woman who looks like she spends most of her time in the garden or drinking tea in a cozy cottage. I find a few books that we can order for her from other libraries and place them on hold.

"Do you know any examples of what different flowers mean?" I ask her since the topic piques my curiosity.

"Well, red roses are obviously for love or romance," she begins, "but I just learned a few more. Daisies mean innocence, orange lilies represent hatred, and purple hyacinths are for sorrow or regret. There's so many more though that I can't wait to learn about."

"That's so fascinating," I say. "You'll have to come back and let me know more of what you learn."

The love I have for this work helps me relax and the tension that has been building up behind my shoulders melts away. At least until I spot Jamie standing at the desk when I walk back from the copy machine a little while later. I immediately think of the language of flowers. Roses for love. Purple hyacinths for regret.

"What can I do for you James?" I ask him with a sigh as bouquets of red and purple fade from my mind.

"I was thinking we could actually start working on the plan for the program."

A lull in the number of people in the library had begun, so it was as good a time as any so I respond, "okay," and we get to work.

It was pretty easy to find examples of other classes online we could pull from so building a basic lesson plan doesn't take very long. When focused on a project, it's not so bad being around Jamie. We work well together as colleagues. If only there was no pesky past between us.

The announcement for the closing of the library heralds the end of the workday and we stop our progress. Grace asks for Jamie's help with a computer that was acting up and I make my escape soon after to grab my stuff and leave. Apparently Jamie knows his IT stuff because he catches up to me in the staff room.

"I really was hoping we could clear the air," he insists as we walk to the parking lot.

"We honestly don't need to. I've moved on Jamie," I call him by his nickname without thinking and curse myself inwardly.

"Please Melody, give me two minutes."

I stop and turn to him. He has his hands out in front of him as if he was offering me something. What does he have to offer me? Closure? Maybe. What if what he tells me only makes me feel worse?

"Fine," I give in.

"Look, I know things didn't end well for us and it was all my fault but I did like you back then and I'm sorry I hurt you. I was just a stupid kid."

"Don't do that. Don't pretend like you didn't know better because you were young. We all make choices. Sometimes those choices hurt people. Take full responsibility or don't bother."

I walk away but Jamie makes the mistake of trying to continue with the conversation.

"Yes, I made a mistake, but I don't understand why you're still so angry about it. It was so long ago."

I can't believe I'm hearing this. Who does he think he is? He breaks my heart, and he thinks he can decide how long I get to be upset about it? The sincerity in his words hit me like a blow to the chest as I realize he truly doesn't understand how much he hurt me.

"Did you cheat on me with Nicole?"

His eyes go wider but his mouth stays in a firm line. Is he shocked I actually asked the question? Did he think I had no idea what he was doing back then?

"Do you really want to know the answer?"

I recall the countless times I laid in his arms. The times I'd never felt closer to any other human being as we touched, kissed, and had sex. How much it meant to me and how each moment made me fall a little bit in love with him.

"Yes. I do."

"Fine," he avoids my gaze and crosses his arms. "I almost did a couple times, but I stopped before it got that far. I'm sure you'd probably think I cheated on you emotionally though."

Rage boils through my chest and spews from my mouth like molten lava.

"Do you want a fucking reward for only *almost* having sex with somebody else while you were dating me? And what do you even mean 'you'd probably think?' Tell any other woman what you did, and they'd probably think you cheated on me emotionally too you asshole. You just had zero regard for me or my feelings. All you could think about was you and your dick and somehow your thought process is, hey at least I didn't *actually* have sex with someone else while dating her! Go me!"

"You just don't get it Mel," he huffs a little and waves me away before turning.

"You're right! I don't!" I yell and I realize I'm still in the library parking lot so I lower my voice and continue. "I thought we had something great, Jamie. God knows I don't want to admit it but I was well on my way to falling in love with you and then you ended it like you did. Like none of it mattered. Like I didn't matter. You know what, fine. Let's leave it at we were young and dumb and call it good. Goodnight Jamie."

"I am so sorry I hurt you Melody," his voice is soft and his pupils bore into mine like he's trying to convey more with those dark brown eyes than with his voice.

"A lot of good that does me now, Jamie," it's my turn to huff, and I shut my car door in his face, done with him and this conversation.

Who does he think he is? I understand us working together was completely random and we need to be professional to tolerate being in the same building every day, but that doesn't mean we need to rehash the past. It solves nothing, and it doesn't magically make me feel better. I'm sure he was probably wanting to make himself feel better after being confronted with his misdeeds after all these years. Making him feel better is not my responsibility. He made his choices, and while they affected me deeply back then, I got to a better place and what matters now is I stay there.

I slam my hands on the steering wheel and let out a shout of frustration. Even though I know I'm right about everything I said, he still makes me want to scream. What's worse is even though his stupid face makes me so angry, I can't deny I'm still unbelievably attracted to him.

His smile still makes me want to melt, and the sight alone of his whole body makes mine go nuts. I obviously haven't seen him without his shirt on at work, but if I had to guess, he probably hasn't let himself go in that area.

Stupid. Stupid. Stupid.

"Why me?" I ask out loud to nobody but the angel and devil on my shoulders.

Still reeling from our less than friendly conversation, I decide there's only one thing that will make me feel better. I grab a huge, piping hot chai tea from my favorite cafe, Brewed Awakening in downtown Vermilion, before heading to Showse Park right on the edge of Lake Erie.

I spent the first eighteen years of my life in Vermilion and only left to go to college in Chicago. For a year or two after graduation, I puttered around the suburbs hoping to find a job in a library there but it didn't work out. I transferred from the Starbucks there to a Starbucks closer to home and I've been here since. If I thought I'd end up getting a job with Jamie so far away from Chicago, I might have tried a little harder to stay there.

Lake Michigan is nice too, but it's not Lake Erie. It's not home. The crashing of the small waves is familiar and tranquil as I sit down on a bench. The breeze is blowing, making the warm late summer air a little less humid. I watch the seagulls fly about, only touching land to eat the scraps left behind by humans. There were a lot of times growing up I'd wish to be a seagull.

"Why would you want to be one of those nasty things?" My mom would scrunch up her nose and shake her head.

"They get to spend all day every day flying high and free in the sky above the lake. What could be better?"

She'd continue to shake her head in confusion but it didn't bother me. I loved their white feathers that made them blend in with the clouds and foam of the crashing waves. Seagulls remind me of home and peace.

Now that I'm sitting here as an adult, the same thing that calmed me as a child brings me relief from my raging thoughts now.

I sip my warm tea and read my current favorite book while getting lost in the sounds of the lake and the words of a magical world different from my own. I try not to admit to myself that the whole time I'm picturing the male hero as a version of Jamie that doesn't let me down.

Chapter 4: Riley Knows Best

As I pull up to my apartment an hour later, my phone vibrates in my pocket. I don't know why I'm so relieved to see it's only Riley. There's no way Jamie still has my number.

"Hey, you, what are you up to?" Riley asks.

"I just got home from wallowing in self-pity at the lake with plans to get in my pajamas and force cuddles on my cat for the rest of the night. Chocolate and the annual start of my Gilmore Girls binge leading into autumn may be involved."

"Well, change those plans 'cause we're going out."

"Not tonight Riley, I'm not in the mood."

I unlock my door and am greeted with soft rubs against my leg by a dark gray fur ball named Lucy. I named her after my favorite character in my favorite childhood book series, *The Chronicles of Narnia.*

"Meow," she announces in her sweet yet demanding voice.

"We both know your automatic feeder already went off," I scold her. "Good try though."

"Come on Mel," Riley scolds me. "We both know it will be good for you."

"I want nothing that's good for me. I want chocolate, extreme introversion, and terrible movies."

"Oh stop being dramatic," I practically hear Riley roll her eyes. "I'll be there in an hour and if you're not dressed in something cute, I'll stop doing movie nights for a month and then we'll see how you do with your 'extreme introversion'."

I'm tempted to call her bluff because being on my own for an entire month doesn't actually sound so bad but I know by the second week I'd be dying for her company.

"Fine," I grumble. "But you'll owe me for this."

"Whatever you say darling best friend," she laughs and hangs up.

"Ugh Luc, why can't people be more like cats? Happy to ignore anything that's not food or a comfy warm spot in the sun."

Instead of spending an hour petting my cat in my coziest pajamas, I find my favorite summer dress and throw it on. Riley calls it my watermelon dress because the top is a reddish pink with little black hearts and the skirt is a flowing light green and white ombre. I can see where she's coming from but that's not why I chose it. I love it because it's so light and flattering with its sweetheart neckline.

Every time I wear it, I want to go dance in a field of flowers soaked in sunshine with the wind blowing through my hair.

I had already done my hair and makeup for work so I was ready to go quicker than I thought. I'm grateful I get to spend at least a few minutes with Lucy before I go. No matter how much time I spend with her, I worry it's not enough and she'll miss me even though I know most cats are perfectly happy being left alone.

I spend ten minutes trying to find her because she's gone into another of her "hide in a random spot the big troll can't find" moods. I find her tucked away under the bed laying on an old purple cardigan I thought I had lost. I *psp psp psp* to get her to come out but she gives me a look that speaks volumes about how pathetic she thinks I am before she lays her head back on her paws.

"Fine, be that way you grumpy thing."

My eyes catch on an old shoebox I forgot I'd thrown under the bed when I moved in. I couldn't bring myself to get rid of it, but I also couldn't leave it in a place where I'd see it all the time. I give Lucy a dirty look wondering if she is actually a mind-reading witch who prefers to spend her time as a cat. Or maybe she's an ordinary feline. I shrug and pull out the box. A deep sigh explodes from me as I open the lid.

Of course that would be the first picture on top. I lift the old polaroid I should most definitely have lit on fire and thrown in a trash can like a dramatic movie heroine. Jamie grew up more than I thought he had. In the picture, his face definitely has a chubbiness he's lost through either age or taking good care of himself. His hair is slightly longer and more unkempt and there's a boyish glint of mischief in his eyes that's transformed into a mature steadiness.

We're standing together on a bridge in Chicago, his arm wrapped around me and we're both smiling like we're having the time of our lives. Was it a fake smile? Was he wishing he had been with Nicole?

I can't help but take in the younger version of me and wonder why I wasn't good enough. Was I not attractive enough? Not cool enough? Why couldn't he feel the same about me?

"What was it like growing up in Chicago?" I asked as we walked across the bridge holding hands.

"I'm sure it can't be that different from your childhood," he said.

"The most exciting thing that happens in my hometown is the annual fish festival. I'm certain living in a place like Chicago is vastly different," I told him.

"Seriously?" He gave me a look of incredulity before throwing his head back and laughing.

"Well, I spent a lot of time with my friends exploring the city. I knew the 'L' like the back of my hand by the time I was ten. School was school. Do you want to see it?"

I wanted to get to know him as much as I could so I said, "absolutely."

We took the train to the other side of the city and when we ended up in front of his school, I burst out laughing.

"You're kidding right?"

"What?" Genuine confusion was written in every feature of his face.

Saint Ignatius College Prep looked like someone plopped Hogwarts out of the English countryside and dropped it in Chicago. It was huge and formidable looking, especially at night.

"My high school looked like a two story brick prison surrounded by corn fields in the middle of nowhere Ohio. This is the fanciest looking high school I've ever seen."

He shifted his weight before folding his arms together and touching his palm to his cheek. Did he not realize how different this school was to most other high schools in America?

"It was a fantastic school," he rubbed the back of his neck. "I was lucky to get a scholarship. Growing up on the west side of Chicago, I never would have thought I'd end up here. Or Oakhaven College."

"It's super cool," I intertwine my arm with his and lean my head on his shoulder. "Just different from what I expected."

He spent the rest of the night telling me more about his childhood, family, and the hijinks he got up to in high school with his friends. It bothered me how often he mentioned Nicole but I kept telling myself, "they're just friends, Melody. Stop making a big deal out of nothing." God, I was such a dumbass.

I consider tearing up the picture and throwing it away but I don't. The same part of me that didn't burn it before still wants it now. Despite the hurt, it's still a nice memory.

"I'm heeeerrreee," Riley belts as she prances through the front door. "You better be ready to go. This is going to be so much fun."

"What are we even doing?" I ask as I make my appearance from the bedroom.

"You look amazing!" Riley hugs me and she's wearing her circle glasses like Simon from Alvin and the Chipmunks. She must be feeling studious today.

"Thank you, but that's not the question I asked," I tease and poke her in the stomach. She's wearing jeans and a fitted blazer over a nice red satin blouse and I feel overdressed in comparison.

"It's a surprise," she smiles with a glint in her eye.

"Ugh." I roll my eyes and she practically drags me out the door, only stopping to let me grab my purse and black flats.

I yell to Lucy I'll be home later as if she'd understand me or even care. She pops her head out from the bedroom and pierces me with her gray-green eyes and I know that's as good as it gets.

"You could at least tell me where we're going," I plea.

"A bar," she says in a teasing voice as she starts her blue Prius.

"Ah yes, very helpful," I roll my eyes.

"Stop it Melody," Riley admonishes. "It'll be fun and you'll have a good time, I promise."

"Okay," I watch out the window as we drive wherever it is we're going.

I always like to pretend I'm in a movie and the window is the movie screen. A documentary on the real world I can view for a little while but don't have to take part in. I can wonder about the people living their lives, completely separate from mine.

In about twenty minutes, Riley pulls up in front of Brewed & Crafty, a craft brewery in Avon, the next town over. The sign outside says, "Open Mic TONIGHT 8 p.m."

"I've heard good things about a band that's playing and thought it'd be fun," Riley says as she parks the car.

"It will be fun," I admit. "Awesome music and great beer sounds perfect right now. Thank you, Riley."

How is it Riley knows what I need before I do? She's so much more than my best friend. She is a sister to me. If I ever have kids, she'll be Aunt Riley.

We head inside and grab a tall table near the stage. Our server delivers our appetizers and drinks; a blackberry ale for me and a local IPA for Riley. I dip the warm and salty German style soft pretzel into their specially made beer cheese and close my eyes at the taste. Talk about comfort food.

I have to stop myself from finishing the entire tray myself as the first act appears on stage. An unassuming woman with a blonde bob hops on stage with a guitar and stands in front of the mic. She kind of reminds me of Tinkerbell in her light green mini dress.

When she opens her mouth to sing, I'm convinced she may actually be a faerie because her voice is so soft and ethereal. She sings a song of a faraway land and a lost romance that would be perfect for a fantasy movie soundtrack. It's beautiful. The whole room stops and becomes silent to hear her song. When she finishes, the entire room comes back to life as though we were all frozen in time to hear her song.

"Wow," Riley says once the singer is off the stage. "She was incredible. I'm going to go grab her information so we can follow her on social."

Once Riley is away from the table, a voice I wasn't expecting to hear grabs my attention.

"Melody, right?" I turn and am surprised by Sebastian standing to my left, giving me a friendly smile.

"Sebastian, right?" I grin back.

"I was looking forward to seeing you at the library again, but fate seems to want to push us together even sooner," he flirts.

"It would seem so," I gesture for him to come sit while Riley's away, knowing she'll see him sitting there and steer clear for a few minutes.

"So, is this typical of how you spend your free time?" he asks with a crooked grin

"Why do you want to know?" I narrow my eyes playfully but maintain my smile hoping I look cute and not dumb.

"Well, I'd love to take you out on a date and if this is what you normally do, it gives me good options for getting it right and making it a night you'll never forget," he runs his hand through that bright red wavy hair and looks down as he chuckles.

"Anything to do with good food, music, or books is a safe bet," I tell him.

"Is that a yes?"

I let his mossy green eyes stare into mine for a second before I bite my lip and nod. From my purse, I pull out the little blue notebook and Sharpie pen I carry with me everywhere. I write my number and rip the sheet out before handing it to him.

"Call me," I tuck my hair behind my ear and smile as coyly as I can.

"Oh I will," he stands and walks away before turning and saying over his shoulder, "that dress looks amazing on you by the way."

I feel my face flush and I know it's got to be a brighter red than his hair.

"Who was that?" Riley asks as she slides into the seat Sebastian vacated.

"A guy I met at the library," I smile and stare off into space, daydreaming about going on a date. "His name is Sebastian. He asked me out."

"Really!" Riley is bouncing in the seat, hands gripped on the edge of the table. "That's so exciting!"

"I know," I squeal as quietly as I can so I don't attract any attention.

"He's cute," she peeks over my shoulder, her eyes trailing him up and down, "and he has a nice butt."

"Stop!" I laugh but peek over as well and am pleased his gaze is already turned toward me.

He winks when his eyes catch mine. Cue more blushing.

"Be careful," Riley warns and I turn back to her in surprise, finding her suddenly serious. "Don't jump into anything unless you honestly think it could be something. Protect your heart."

"I'll be fine," I reassure her but disbelief is clear in the way her eyebrows are raised and her head tilted.

A comedian who is not as funny as he thinks he is comes on next. His "jokes" mostly consist of shouting random phrases and hopping all over the stage chaotically. He's followed by a young black poet who performs a moving and beautiful spoken word about her identity and fitting into the world. The band Riley wanted to see comes on after.

The group features an acoustic guitarist with spiky blonde hair, a keyboard player who appears better suited to a golf course than a stage in his sporty blue polo, and a young Asian singer with long black hair that is extremely contrasting to her bright pink miniskirt and matching halter top.

"Why did the pianist keep banging his head against the keys?" the keyboardist asks the audience and waits for a response that doesn't come. "He was playing by ear!"

There are a few chuckles and quiet laughs in the audience but the biggest reaction comes from Riley who starts cracking up, drawing looks from everyone close to our vicinity.

"What?" It's her turn to blush now when she realizes no one else is laughing as much as she is. "It was funny!"

The keyboardist notices Riley's reaction and is immediately enraptured by her. Maybe I should try to introduce her to him after the performance. The song they play is pretty good but not my cup of tea. It reminded me a lot of the pop punk that used to be popular when we were in high school. Though the members of the band are mismatched in the way you wouldn't expect to find them hanging out at the mall together, they end up meshing super well and the crowd is pretty into it.

More music acts follow. Riley stops after her first drink so she can drive home while I have three more blackberry ales and end up much drunker than I thought I would be tonight. I spend more time trying to catch glimpses of Sebastian on the other side of the bar than pay attention to the performances.

He's sitting with a much stockier dude whose bleach blond hair can't be natural. I don't let my gaze linger enough to gain more than a general vibe they might be close because they spend a lot of time laughing. Sebastian often runs his hand through his hair and when he laughs, it's a whole body laugh that makes him bend and clutch his stomach. Glancing over my shoulder, I'm able to appreciate his looks more discreetly. I gathered he was taller than me at the library which is amazing. He's got a bit of chubbiness around the center, but not unhealthily, more like he appreciates a good meal but knows how to keep fit. His arms are the kind of thick that are perfect for wrapping around someone in a cozy and comforting cuddle. Or hauling them over their shoulder to carry to bed.

Maybe this could be my chance at love. He seems so nice and has at least a couple similar interests to me. I could definitely see us together.

My mind immediately conjures an image of Jamie and me. My failing inhibitions cause me to say, "go away Jamie," out loud and Riley makes a funny face at me like I'm losing it.

"Okay, I think that's our cue to head out," Riley runs to the bar to pay our tab and my body moves before I actually give it permission to.

Before I know it, I'm standing in front of Sebastian.

"You're a nice guy right?" There's a slight slur to my words and sober Mel is screaming from the pits of my brain to shut up and leave, but drunk Mel has other ideas.

"I like to think so," he smiles and I giggle like a schoolgirl.

"Good," I give what is probably not as cute a smile as I would like and flick my hair like I've seen other hot young girls do. "Don't forget to call me."

"I won't," he winks again and my heart does a small flutter.

In my mind, I float out the door on a little cloud; I'm pretty sure in real life, Riley grabs me by the shoulder and pulls me out the door.

"Wow," Riley laughs as she helps me in the car. "You're gonna be so mad about that tomorrow morning."

"I had such a good time Riley," I lay my head on the cold window as she drives out of the parking lot. "I love you so much. Thank you for being my best friend."

"I love you too Mel," she quickly rests her head on my shoulder and then focuses back on the road.

"Do you really think he likes me?" A whimper comes into my voice and even drunk me is mad I'm getting all weepy about this.

"I certainly hope he does," she consoles me. "I don't think he would have asked you out if he didn't."

"I hope he doesn't break my heart like Jamie," I mutter. "Stupid Jamie. Why does he have to be attractive still? He's hot and annoying. It's not fair."

"I know honey," she rubs my arm. "I'm sure things with Sebastian will work out and you'll be able to move on from Jamie for good."

"You better be right," I pout.

I nod off for the rest of the drive and before I know it we're back in front of my apartment.

Riley's staying the night so she helps me out of the car with my arm wrapped around her waist. We make our way to the stairs to get to my front door.

"It's a nice night," I stop walking and the loss of momentum pulls Riley back with me. "Can we look at the stars for a minute?"

"Sure," she sits on a cement curb block in a parking spot and I plop down next to her so I can crane my neck to appreciate the unfathomable night sky.

I sigh loudly and then I'm quit, my head resting on her shoulder and her head stacked on top of mine. I pretend for a moment we're alone in the universe and it's just us and the stars. There's no such thing as stupid boys and heartbreak.

After about ten minutes, we silently agree to stand and head inside.

"Wait," I pause again and Riley furrows her brow and pinches her lips. "I feel like there's someone watching us."

We both scan the parking lot and I feel the hairs on my arms stand straight as goosebumps spread from my shoulder to wrist. There are a bunch of dark cars and lights on in other apartments but no other human being to be found.

"I don't feel anything," Riley says, clearly creeped out.

"I'm sure it's nothing then," I shake my head and lead her inside. "It's probably just the alcohol getting to me."

I hope I convinced Riley because I sure didn't convince myself. The feeling lingers even once I'm inside my apartment. I lock the door and the deadbolt and close all my blinds before settling in for the night, hoping I never get a feeling like that again.

Chapter 5: Butterflies

"Good morning Grace," I greet my boss in the sweetest voice I can when I have a headache more akin to a jackhammer pounding directly on my skull.

"Good morning Melody," she grins at me and walks away, stops, and says "Oh, by the way, our other librarian who's been on vacation is back today. His name is Jackson. He'll be with you at the information desk. Let's go meet him."

I follow Grace to the staff workroom and am surprised by a familiar face.

"You were the keyboardist in the band last night!"

Jackson is wearing a purple polo this morning but other than that, it's definitely the same guy. He blinks at me a few times making it obvious he definitely doesn't recognize me.

"You were at Brewed & Crafty? What did you think of the song?"

"You guys were great. My best friend Riley wanted to see you guys perform. She was the one who laughed super hard at your piano joke in the beginning."

Recognition sparks in his eyes and he snaps his fingers followed by fingers guns in confirmation he remembers.

"I'll leave you guys to it!" Grace bows out and heads to her office.

"So you're Melody the new girl," he comments as we walk to the information desk.

"So you're Jackson the librarian moonlighting as a keyboardist," I counter. "It was a cool song."

"Thank you," he says. "Are you new to town as well?"

"I grew up in Vermilion but went to college outside of Chicago before coming back to the area a couple years ago."

"Very cool. Do you want to be a librarian?"

"That's the dream," I sit down next to him at the desk and pull up my work email.

We talk a little and he tells me he grew up in Colorado and got his Master's in Library Science from the University of Denver before getting the job here a year ago. He tells me he loves playing keyboard with his band which he reminds me is called PunnyNotFunny, hence the slightly better than terrible pun at the beginning.

"I play a lot of golf."

"That explains the polos," I tease a little. "Do you have a library specialty?"

"Historical non-fiction but I'm pretty good with historical fiction too because that's what I read for fun."

"Awesome," I tell him. "I'm a big genres person. Give me a good fantasy, mystery, or romance and I'm your gal."

"Don't you get tired of the tropes?"

"Absolutely not! I find it comforting and ridiculously satisfying when a story goes the way it's supposed to."

We go back to our own work for a bit, each of us helping different patrons when Jackson says, "I haven't met the new IT guy. Jamie right? Know anything about him?"

A "ha!" almost explodes from my mouth but I hold it in. "A little," is the response I go with instead.

"Is he a good guy?"

What a question. Do I personally think he's a good guy? Not really. Do I think he's generally a good guy to most other people and is good at his job? Yeah, I guess.

"He's fine. Jamie's good at his job."

"Thank you Melody," Jamie says from behind me.

Goddammit. How does he keep sneaking up on me like that?

"Speak of the devil," I grumble and turn back to my computer. "Did you need something Jamie?"

Jackson raises his eyebrows in confusion since I just said Jamie was fine and now I'm acting like I want nothing to do with him. The two are definitely not mutually exclusive.

"I thought we could work on our program for a little while."

"Okay," I grumble and log off my computer.

Our last talk still rings in my head and all I want to do is bury my head under a pillow beneath an enormous pile of blankets. Maybe I can't do this. When I get home, I'm going to go back to searching for other library jobs. It'll probably take a while until I actually find something but at least I'll get away from this situation as soon as humanly possible. Jamie needs to get back in my past where he belongs.

We head to one of the study rooms so we can work without disturbing other patrons or Jackson. I sit down at the head of the table. Although it makes sense for Jamie to sit in the chair kitty corner to me, I wish he was on the opposite side of the table instead.

"For the third and fourth sessions, I was thinking we'd get into the nitty gritty of internet safety," Jamie begins. "Just last week I heard about someone getting scammed out of thousands of dollars by calling a bad number they found online."

"Sure," I nod my head, grateful he starts actually working and not digging into our argument.

"I was also thinking about asking Grace if at the last session we could make a sign-up sheet for more individualized help sessions. Kind of like Geek Squad."

"That's a good idea," I say and mean it.

We go over the plan for the last two sessions and start making power points. As good as he is with technology, his creative skills are lacking and his first slide is black text on a white screen.

"Why don't you let me do this part," I say as I slide the computer in front of me.

I add a pleasant background and insert fun little graphics before making the font a little more interesting than Times New Roman. Jamie watches me work without saying anything but nods here and there to show his approval. His eyes keep flickering to my face and I wonder why.

"I'm sorry our conversation got a little out of hand last night," Jamie says after a few minutes, answering my question.

"It's fine Jamie," I keep my eyes glued to the screen. "Let's just both move on with our lives. The past is the past."

"It's just that I didn't say things the way I meant to say them," his eyebrows furrow and his mouth scrunches. "I got defensive and lost sight of why I wanted to talk in the first place. I'm sorry."

He's staring down at his hands as they rub together. It occurs to me at that moment that I don't hate Jamie. I definitely don't like him but I know deep down he's a guy who made bad choices and is not a bad person.

"It's okay," he glances at me and for a moment I get lost in his brown eyes and almost forget why he was apologizing in the first place. "I'm sorry I yelled at you."

"I kinda deserved it didn't I?" he gives a half smile and my icy heart melts a little.

"A little," I smile back and I wonder if finding a new job will be necessary after all.

"So what have you been up to the last few years," he asks.

"I tried to get a library job in Chicago but there wasn't a ton available and they're in super high demand. So I got a job at Starbucks and worked in Oakbrook before moving back here a couple years ago. I kept working at Starbucks before getting the job here. Not very exciting I know. What about you?"

"I stayed close to home and got a job at a tech company in the city after graduation. I stayed there until I decided I needed a change and found the job here."

"Yeah, you never said exactly what prompted that?"

"It's a long story," he repeats the same thing as when I first asked him and studies his hands, making me much more curious than I should be. "I just needed a change."

Vague much? I want to ask more. Ask about Nicole and if he dated anyone else serious or not. What made him leave his home for a nowhere place in northern Ohio. I don't pry though. It's none of my business.

"What are some fun things to do around here?" He changes the subject.

"Um," I laugh. "Compared to Chicago, probably not a ton. Going to Lake Erie with friends is fun when it's warm. Especially if you have boat friends which I don't. There are some good bars and restaurants. Last night my best friend Riley and I went to one called Brewed & Crafty in Avon. Luckily Cleveland's not too far away if you're looking for more city type fun. You just have to be down to drive an hour."

"I'm actually looking to slow down a little from city life," he comments to my surprise. "I'll have to check out that bar."

"It was cool. They had an open mic night, and I saw from their calendar they do other stuff like trivia nights and karaoke. Jackson, the librarian, is a keyboardist who played last night. It was funny, I actually ran into that patron Sebastian there too and he asked me out."

Jamie's posture straightens, and his eyes narrow. I forgot Jamie said he didn't like Sebastian and that Jamie and I aren't actually friends who talk about things like this. Am I an idiot? It's a wonder I get anything done when I keep doing stupid shit like this. Deep down though I know it's because I feel like I have something to prove to Jamie. That some guys want me and that he made a mistake.

"Really?" he says. "What did you say?"

I feel like that's a trick question but I don't owe him anything other than honesty so I tell him I said yes.

"I really didn't like that guy Mel."

"Good thing it's none of your business Jamie," I roll my eyes. "I don't even know why I said anything. Let's just get back to work."

"I just don't think it's a good idea," he continues on.

"It's not your responsibility to think anything about him or the situation. Why do you even care?"

I glare at him and he stares back, his mouth opens a bit as if he wants to say something but doesn't know what. He stutters but words don't come out.

"That's what I thought," I get back to my presentation and keep my mouth shut.

Stupid. Stupid. Stupid. *Don't let your guard down Melody. He's your ex. A coworker now. Not your friend. Get through this stupid program and then you can pretend he doesn't exist or get a new job.*

We finish up quickly with as little communication as possible. Jamie slinks back to his office and I go back to the information desk to finish up the workday. Hopefully, in peace from Jamie and his incessant need to try to be friends with me.

"You said you only know a little about him?" Jackson asks as I sit down with a knowing smile.

"We may have a little history," I admit reluctantly. "Ancient history. It's been a long time since I knew him."

"If you say so," he turns back to his computer. "So, about your friend. Riley you said?"

"Yes," I turn back to him and he's blushing.

"Would she happen to be single?"

"She would. Would you like me to give her your number?"

"Yes, thank you," he grins from ear to ear and I'm suddenly in a much better mood.

As soon as I get to my car after work I call Riley.

"You'll never guess who my other coworker is," I say when she answers the phone.

"Oh no, not this again. Don't tell me it's another one of your exes. Now that really would be a bad movie plot."

"Do you remember the piano player you lost your shit over last night?"

"You can't be serious."

"He's a librarian named Jackson who likes history, golf, and puns. He wanted me to give you his number!"

"Holy shit!" excitement coats her voice, which has gone up about two octaves.

"I'll text it to you once I get home. How was the coffee shop?"

"I had this lady lose it on me because we ran out of almond milk," she groaned.

"Again?"

"People are passionate about their almond milk," she sighs. "Just one day I'd like to go without someone getting mad at me because I don't make their drink fast enough, or it's not hot enough, or it's too hot."

"I know. Have you had any luck in your job search?"

"A couple leads, but nothing's panned out yet. Keep your fingers crossed for me."

"Always. I gotta go, I'm getting another call from a number I don't know. Text me if you need anything. Love you!"

"Love you!" She hangs up and I answer the incoming call.

"Hello?"

"Melody? It's Sebastian. How are you?"

I hold in a squeal and take a deep breath before responding with, "I'm great. I'm so glad you called."

"Me too," his smooth voice says from somewhere far away but feels so close over the speakers in my car. "Are you busy tonight?"

While I try not to shout in excitement, Sebastian and I make plans to meet up at a French bistro at 7:30. I push the speed limit getting the rest of the way home so I can take a shower and get ready all over again. It's cooler tonight so I grab my long black skirt with a slit up the leg and a red long sleeve blouse with a deep neckline I tuck into the hem of the skirt. I throw on my black fitted jacket and mousse my hair into gentle waves.

If only one strand didn't decide to go rogue and be super curly for no reason at all. I consider cutting the strand off entirely but know that will probably make my hair look worse. I tuck it behind my ear and hope it stays there.

I arrive at the restaurant, Bon Manger, ten minutes early and spend the entire time in the car checking my makeup and hair, more nervous than I've been in a while. In the few dates I've gone on since Jamie, there was no one I had a strong connection with. Even the guy I went out with for a month last year was fun but nothing special. I pull together every shred of confidence I can and jump out of the car.

"Melody," Sebastian calls as I'm almost to the entrance.

I turn around and am impressed by how good he looks, clearly pulling out all the stops. If I had to guess, he recently got his hair cut and styled, his gorgeous red hair gelled perfectly in place, his bangs coiffed just so it appears like an effortless wave. He's wearing dark wash fitted jeans with a forest green paisley button-up shirt matching his eyes perfectly.

"Hi," I say as he catches up to me. "I'm so glad you called."

"Not as much as I am," he opens the door for me as chivalrous as one can be and we head inside. "I'm not going to lie; it took a bit of working up to because I was so nervous."

"You were nervous?" I ask incredulously after he talks to the host.

We get seated at a small table in a corner with a dark red tablecloth and a candle in the center.

"Incredibly nervous," he chuckles. "I'd be crazy not to be, given how beautiful you are."

"Wow," I find my shoelaces, my face aflame. "Thank you. You don't look so bad yourself."

Browsing the menu, I'm at a complete loss of what to get because it all sounds so good. The Boeuf Bourguignon sounds amazing with its rich red wine beef stew and roasted potatoes but I've never tried a real Ratatouille and I've wanted to ever since I saw the Pixar movie.

"What are you thinking of getting?" I ask Sebastian as he stares intently at the menu.

"I was thinking about the Steak au Poivre," I find it on the menu myself and think it'd sound pretty good if I liked steak. Whatever I get, I know I won't go home regretting my choice.

In the end, I decide on the Boeuf Bourguignon and Sebastian orders the steak. We both request a dark red wine to accompany our meals and then we're left to our own devices until our meal comes.

"So you know I work at a library, what do you do for work?"

"I'm a sales guy," he says. "I head up the sales department for a local manufacturing warehouse."

"Wow," I try to think of what to say but come up blank. "That sounds so interesting!"

"It isn't," he laughs, "but thanks for trying. I'm guessing acting is not in your background?"

"Uh," now it's my turn to run my hand through my hair. "Definitely not. Do you enjoy your work?"

"I do. I've always been good at talking to people and the product is good so it's an easy sell. Growing up everyone said I'd be a great salesman, so I thought, why fight it? Do you enjoy working at the library?"

"Oh I love it," I gush and ramble on because I could talk about libraries and how amazing they are for hours. "Libraries are my genuine passion and I've been dreaming of working at a library for as long as I can remember. Obviously, books and reading are a big part of it but there are so many amazing resources libraries provide to their community. Did you know we're starting a seed library? It's so cool. Patrons can come get five seed packets a month and grow their own food right in their backyard! I've heard of other libraries having musical instruments and tools available to check out. There's computer access, printing and copying, public programs, literally so many wonderful things that genuinely help so many people."

I pause because he's giving me a funny look. "What?"

"It's fun to listen to someone talk about things that matter to them. I just think you're incredible."

"Goodness," I've never had anyone say something like that to me. "Thank you so much. What are you passionate about?"

He thinks for a second, hand on his chin before stating, "sports."

Not exactly what I thought he'd say but I'm curious so I respond with, "why are you passionate about sports?"

"They teach people a lot of valuable lessons like teamwork, leadership, exercising, losing at something, and most of all they're fun."

"What's your favorite sport?"

"Football."

At his response, I try to picture myself as the girlfriend of a sports lover. Will we dress up in his favorite team's jerseys and have watch parties? Should I learn the rules of football? Or baseball? Or every sport?

"I'm not gonna lie, I know nothing about sports."

"That's okay, I don't know enough about books so you teach me that and I'll teach you about sports."

"Perfect."

The rest of the date is great. Sebastian and I learn more about each other and have no problem finding conversations. He grew up near Columbus so of course his favorite team is the Ohio State Buckeyes. He wasn't kidding when he said he loves sports because I learn more about football, baseball, and basketball in the short time with him than I have in my whole life. I also learn he's a dog person, and he has a golden retriever named Blaze. I think for a moment it might be an issue because I'm the exact opposite of a dog person, but it's not an issue I need to worry about on a first date.

"What's your favorite book?" he asks once we've both finished our meals and debated on dessert.

"That's such a hard question," I put my napkin on the table and sip my water, having stopped with the wine after the first glass. "One I don't think I can answer. It honestly depends on my mood and the day. I have a lot of favorites for a lot of different reasons."

"I hope you'll educate me on some good ones I should check out on our next date," he not so subtly inquires.

"I would love to," I respond and he grins like I gave him the best birthday gift he's ever received.

When the check comes, panic about how we might say goodbye grips my nerves. Is he going to kiss me? Will he want more? Will he walk me to my car or will we part at the door? I've done pretty good on this date so far, but it would definitely be right on par for me to embarrass myself in the last five minutes.

He pays without hesitation and I thank him for such a nice date. "It was lovely, thank you Sebastian."

"Thank you for agreeing to go out with me. When can we do it again?"

We walk to the front door, giving me a second to think about my response. "This weekend?"

"Perfect," he smiles at me when we walk outside and I notice for the first time how when he smiles he's only got one dimple on the left side. "I'll call you tomorrow?"

"Sounds great."

There's a moment of hesitation where neither of us know how to proceed. Sebastian decides first and leans down and I spend five milliseconds freaking out thinking he's going to kiss me. I'm frozen. Instead of heading for my mouth, he tilts his head and his lips land gently on my cheek as a soft caress.

"I'll talk to you soon," I say softly and scurry to my car.

Rebekah Santoro

Chapter 6: Rose

Weeks go by and life settles into a sense of normalcy. Jamie and I only talk when we're preparing for the program, but we did so much work in the beginning there's not too much left to do until it starts.

Sebastian and I only go on two more dates during this time as he had to suddenly fly to California to say goodbye to his grandfather and attend his funeral. The dates have gone well. I wouldn't say it's true love but I'm enjoying getting to know him and hope with more time spent together, the more it can become.

At the end of each date, he stuck with the sweet cheek kisses. I'm keeping my fingers crossed that at the end of our next date, I'll get a proper kiss and really test how things feel between us. I'm also debating with myself how I feel about sleeping with him. In the dates I've gone on in the last few years, I've had a couple flings but it's been long enough I'm ridiculously nervous to start that kind of relationship with anybody.

The day of the first session of Technology 101 for Seniors dawns and I'm dreading spending time with Jamie. It's been nice he's finally giving the both of us space from each other. I guess our last two conversations finally got through to him.

Jackson spends a lot of the day telling me his best puns in between patron questions and I'd say about fifty percent of them actually get me laughing. According to Sebastian, fifty percent is a pretty good batting average so in baseball terms, his pun telling skills are great.

"What did the grape say when it got crushed?" Jackson asked after he helped a patron renew his library card privilege. "Nothing, it just let out a little wine."

He cracks himself up and I even laugh a little at that one. A few older patrons walk in the library and start heading toward the meeting room where we're hosting the class. I glance at the clock and it's about time for the program to begin. I let Jackson know where I'm going and he shouts another pun as a farewell gift.

"Hey Mel," he says, "I knew a guy who collected candy canes; they were all in mint condition."

I turn around to give him shit for the terrible pun and almost slam directly into Jamie's firm form.

"Jesus," I throw my hands up and they automatically land on his chest.

"You can just call me Jamie," he teases.

I can't even lie to myself. Jamie's chest feels nice. It's so solid and my hands fit perfectly on his pecs. For a quick moment, I picture myself laying my head down and listening to his heartbeat, like I did so many times before. I quickly remind myself it was a false sense of security and no matter how nice his chest feels, I need to stay far away from it.

"Hilarious," I throw my hands back down by my side and take two steps backward. "Sorry for bumping into you."

"No problem. Are you ready to get started?"

"As I'll ever be," I sweep my arm in front of me so he can lead the way and I follow him into the meeting room.

The few folks who have already arrived have each chosen a computer to sit at and appear to have varying levels of confusion. An older gentleman who looks like he could be a mall Santa at Christmastime is at the first computer and is glaring at the screen as though his attendance was coerced. My guess is the older woman with long brown hair sitting beside him is his wife who made him come, given the way she keeps talking to him in reassuring tones.

The third person in the room is an older black gentleman with salt and pepper hair who brought a *Computers for Seniors* book along with him and is already pulling up a web browser when I walk behind him.

Right as I reach the front of the room, a new group of seniors walks in. The first two are an older Hispanic couple who are speaking fluent Spanish and I wonder if Jamie can understand them. When we were dating, he told me even though he is half black and half Mexican, he can only understand Spanish conversationally and doesn't speak it.

Behind the couple is the kind of older woman you see and immediately think "fun Grandma." She's not actually your grandma but you'd want her to be your honorary one who gives you sage advice and lots of sweets. She's got rosy cheeks and a kind smile. Her white hair falls down to the middle of her back in a braid and she's wearing tan pants and a lavender blouse. She looks so kind and inviting and I have a hunch she's probably a superb cook.

"Hello there!" She greets everyone, and the entire room responds as though they know her.

She picks a computer in the very center of the room so she can talk to everybody. She immediately strikes up a conversation with the Hispanic couple and speaks fluent Spanish too, even though I would have never guessed since she appears as white as me.

Two more seniors trickle in and then it's time to start the class. I introduce myself first and then Jamie. The nerves that usually come with speaking in front of an audience aren't as high as usual and I wonder if it's because a group of seniors is less intimidating than younger people or because I'm actually getting less anxious. Definitely the first.

Since the group will be together for multiple sessions, we give the participants time to say who they are and their comfortability level with technology.

Almost all of them have basic knowledge but the running theme is technology has changed so much in such a short time they're all confused by the new and different ways of doing things.

"What happened to Internet Explorer?" Santa, A.K.A. Gerald asks when he introduces himself.

"They stopped running it and now the browser on their devices is Microsoft Edge," Jamie answers. "Don't worry, we'll be going over the different browsers you'll likely see and their key features."

Gerald nods but his hands are still balled into fists as he glares at the screen.

I learn the woman I'd love to make my honorary grandma is Rose Chapman, and she wants help using Facebook to stay in touch with her kids & grandkids.

"Good to know," I make a note of both her and Gerald's requests and wait for the rest of the group's introductions.

Jamie begins the program by going over the basic names and uses of the laptop in front of him while going over what it would look like on a desktop version. Then it's my turn to discuss the different programs they might use on the computer. I stick to the different browsers, email platforms, and things like the Microsoft Suite and Google Drive.

The seniors ask lots of minor questions like when Rose wonders "why does a little box with lots of options pop up when I hit the mouse sometimes but not every time?"

"When you click the right side of the mouse that will pop up. It's called a right click. It will allow you to do things like copy, paste, and more depending on where you're selecting," I explain. "When you use your mouse, you'll want to use the left button to select things and the right to see those options when you hover over a link or page. Does that make sense?"

I demonstrate on the big screen mirroring my computer but only about half of the room nods their heads like they understand. The rest are deer caught in headlights.

By the end of the hour, I feel confident the seniors learned some things but seem as confused as when they walked in if not more so. It was a good thing we made this a series of programs and not just one day. I wave goodbye as they file out. I notice Jamie talking to Santiago and Julietta in Spanish before they leave and want to ask him about it but remember it's none of my business.

"Maybe you can help me with something sweetie," Rose catches my attention.

"Of course, what can I do for you?"

"I was hoping you could help me find books or resources on good hobbies for seniors."

"Absolutely, I can," I smile and lead her back to the information desk. "Was there a specific hobby you were looking to start?"

"Nothing in particular. My youngest son moved to New York not too long ago and I haven't been seeing my other kids or grandkids as much as I used to now they're growing up and I need something to do with my time. I refuse to wither away to nothing in my old age. I was a single mom for so long that any hobbies I had before I became a mom I've long since forgotten."

"What are some things you're interested in?" I sit down at my computer and start googling. "The Lorain Senior Center seems to have a lot of great resources and events."

"To be honest, I've always been curious about learning how to draw," she admits while ringing her hands.

"Well, we can definitely find something for that," I reassure her.

I pull up a lot of online pages on the basics of drawing and mention YouTube will be a great place for that.

"We can definitely go over YouTube a bit during our class next week so you can get more comfortable with it. For now, why don't I take you back to our non-fiction section to show you our books on drawing?"

"That sounds great," she follows me to the back of the library and I show her the 741.2 section of our shelves and point out a few possibilities.

"We can always order in books from other libraries too if you're not finding exactly what you're looking for."

"Thank you sweetie," she grins at me. "This is really helpful. You're new here right? I've been coming here for ages and I don't think I've seen you before."

"I started about a month ago."

"So what's your story? What brought you here?"

"I grew up in Vermilion," I tell her. "Then I went to college outside of Chicago. I've been trying to get a job in a library for years but it didn't work out there so I moved home two years ago and finally got this job a month or so ago."

"How wonderful," she pulls a couple books from the shelf. "I've lived in Lorain my whole life but I love Vermilion. There's nothing better than being on Lake Erie if you ask me."

"I tend to agree. Although Lake Michigan was pretty nice too and didn't have a reputation of catching on fire."

"That was such a long time ago," she waves her hand in dismissal. "My kids and I loved sitting by the shore in summer while they were growing up."

"How many kids do you have?"

"Three," she stares off in the distance, fondly thinking of her children. "My oldest, Mary, lives in Cincinnati with her son Aiden. My middle son, Jeffrey, lives in Michigan but he's still a bachelor, and my youngest John recently moved to the northeast with his wife and two kids, twins Morgan and Mallory. I miss them."

"Do they visit often?"

"Not as often as I'd like," she frowns but literally turns it upside down as she continues, "and that's why I want to find a lot of stuff to do on my own."

"We can definitely help with that. We have a lot of great programs too. I think we're having an art club starting later this month."

We pull a few more books for her to experiment with drawing. While we're walking away from the stacks, Rose's eye catches a book on writing and she grabs that as well with the comment, "Maybe I'll write my life story."

As Rose leaves, she tells me she'll be back soon and I find myself excited because I genuinely enjoyed talking to her. Maybe I have my first favorite patron. True to her word, Rose comes back the day after next and she shows me some of her first attempts at drawing.

"These aren't half bad Rose!" I examine her landscape of Lake Erie and while it's not perfect, it's definitely a good first try.

"I sat on a bench in Lakeview park for three hours trying to capture that," she points to the paper. "Next time I'm just trying an apple."

"No! You've got to keep trying the hard stuff until you're amazing at it!"

"Honey, I'll be long dead by the time I could be amazing at anything new," she says with a sardonic laugh. "And that's okay. I came to terms with not doing everything I want before I die a long time ago."

"Well, it never hurts to try does it?" I challenge.

"No, I suppose not."

A sudden need to help this woman enjoy every bit of life overcomes me. I'm not sure why I feel like I have to make this my personal mission, but I do. Maybe it's because I have my share of regret and the idea of myself facing death and living with so many wishes and wants unachieved is scary. Maybe it's because she's a sweet old lady. It doesn't really matter. Something's calling me to befriend Rose and who am I to question fate like that?

"I can help you."

"That's real sweet honey but you must have better things to do, young thing like you."

"I've got time."

Rose visits the library almost every day we're open over the next two weeks. Between that and our program, she quickly becomes one of my friends. Jamie and I continue our silently agreed on plan of only speaking to each other when we're talking about, or teaching, our program or other library stuff. Three sessions down, five to go.

Sebastian comes back to town and we go on two more dates. He took me mini putt-putt golfing on the first and we ended it with an actual kiss. He let me win, purposely missing easy shots on the last few holes. The sun had been setting, and we were holding hands as we walked out. When we got to my car, I was so excited. He leaned down for a kiss and it was...

Fine.

It wasn't a bad kiss. It wasn't the best kiss I've ever had in my life either. The kiss was completely...fine. The worst part is, Sebastian acted like it was amazing. I even think he blushed. I did my best to make it seem like I was totally swooning but when I got in the car, I couldn't hold it in, so I called Riley.

"It wasn't anything to write home about," I told her.

"How disappointing," she said.

"Maybe that's how it's supposed to be though. It's not a movie. It's real life. Passion isn't always a guarantee. Maybe the best you can hope for is that a kiss isn't bad, and the sex is at least good. Maybe passion is overrated."

"That's depressing Mel. And a lot of maybe's."

"It's definitely still worth giving it a shot. It could be better the next time."

"Kinda doubt that but you do you Mel."

Unfortunately, it was the same on our next date to the movies. Except he wanted to make out. He took me to a horror movie, because of course he did. He wrapped his arm around me, probably hoping I'd get scared and curl into his embrace and beg to be comforted with kisses. It was minutes and minutes of just fine kissing. I'm loath to admit it, but I got bored and slightly annoyed because I had become interested in the movie and wanted to find out what happens.

Still, he's such a nice guy, and it feels like a stupid minor thing to get caught up on. The more I get to know him and the more time we spend together, I'm sure the kissing will only get better. Maybe it takes more than a couple dates.

"Have you ever been with a man who wasn't the best kisser?" I ask Rose when she comes in the next day.

"Yes," she snarls. "Run."

"Really?" I ask, completely taken aback.

"You should want to be kissed by the person you love all the time. If he doesn't make you want to do that, then it's not worth sticking around to find out what else he isn't good at."

I don't know what to say in response. Rose clearly speaks from experience and part of me immediately wants to take her advice given her insistence, but the other part keeps going back to giving Sebastian a chance. It's entirely possible I'm a terrible kisser. Who am I to judge?

"Hey Rose," Jamie pops up next to her at the desk with his winning smile and I hold in a groan.

"Jamie!" she practically swoons and I want to roll my eyes. "How are you?"

"Doing just fine. What are we talking about?"

"Melody was just asking about bad kissing," Rose blurts out before I can interject and I immediately hope I'll spontaneously drop dead. Or at least fall into a deep, dark abyss or trans-dimensional portal that is only one way.

"Oh, really?" Jamie turns to me with a smirk. "Having an unpleasant experience Mel?"

"Not currently," I bite back. "I was thinking of the past."

It's a complete lie. I loved kissing Jamie. A lot. Even given my lack of experience, it's the relationship I would say I felt the most passion in. That's not something he needs to know though. It would only remind us both how delusional I was about our entire relationship.

Jamie has the audacity to look offended and I let out a satisfied "hmph." Rose turns her head back and forth between the two of us, curiosity lighting up her eyes but she doesn't bring voice to her thoughts.

"Guess I should get back to work," Jamie waves and as he walks away he says, "I look forward to seeing you at the next class, Rose."

"You as well Jamie," she stares me down as she responds to him and then continues to me with, "that was interesting."

"What was?" I play dumb.

"Hmm," Rose goes back to flipping through the catalog of the other events the library's hosting. "I just love fall. There's so many fun things to do. Although I never seem to do enough of it. I remember when the kids were little, we'd go out to the country every year to go pick apples and then we'd make homemade apple pie and cider. Oh, it was wonderful."

"That sounds so fun. We went apple picking once or twice when I was a kid but it's been a long time."

Then a thought occurs to me and I'm so excited to ask, "What if we went Rose?"

"Went where?" She tilts her head quizzically.

"Apple picking!" I sit down in front of my computer and start googling. "It looks like there's a place called Burnham

Orchards in Berlin Heights that has great reviews for apple picking."

"You don't have to Melody," Rose looks away and tucks her purse higher on her shoulder. "You don't need to waste your time with me!"

"I think you're fun and kind Rose, why wouldn't I want to hang out with you? We can go this weekend."

"You're sure?" she turns her focus back to me, hope lighting up her eyes.

"Absolutely. I'll pick you up Saturday morning. Promise me you'll help make the apple pie because I'm hopeless in the kitchen."

"I can do that," she smiles the biggest, toothiest smile I've ever seen and we cement our plans.

Chapter 7: Apple Picking for the Soul

"Oh, I'm just so excited," Rose says for the third time as she climbs into the car.

"I'm excited too," I pull away from her cute little cottage that sits across the street from Lake Erie and begin driving south-west into the countryside.

As we go, she tells me all sorts of stories about the places we pass. Most of them featured her children and/or grandchildren but a couple also mention her husband. I listen for the most part but find myself wondering about him. She's only mentioned him once or twice but I immediately think he might be the man that prompted her "run" response.

"Is apple pie your favorite?" I ask Rose when there's a pause in her storytelling.

"My favorite depends on the season. Apple pie in fall, chocolate pecan in the winter, rhubarb or cherry in spring, and key lime in summer. I know apple can go with any season, but for me it's always in autumn."

"Wow, I wasn't expecting such a quick and certain opinion on pie."

"I take my pie very seriously," she teases. "So do you and Jamie have a history?"

"I'm not sure what you're talking about," I focus on the road.

"Don't play coy young lady. It was as obvious as a monkey in a boardroom."

"What?"

Rose stares at me, waiting for a response to her original question.

"It's ancient history," I say. "We dated in college. It didn't end very well."

"And now you work together? That's unfortunate."

"You're telling me," I scoff.

"He's so sweet though!" Rose clasps her hands together.

"Oh yes," I shake my head, "sweet until he decides to take your heart out of your chest and stomp on it maniacally like a super evil villain set on destroying everyone's souls."

"Goodness."

"That was dramatic, but the point stands," I say. "I'm trying to pretend he doesn't exist and get through this program with him. I'm even looking into other jobs at libraries in the surrounding area because I don't know if I can handle it long term."

"You can't do that!" she pouts, "You're my new favorite staff member! Even if Jamie is nice to look at!"

"Rose!"

"Oh, you know it's true," Rose pats my leg. "A breakup doesn't make him ugly. Physically at least."

"I know," I grip the steering wheel tighter. "It makes everything so much harder."

As I enter a roundabout and veer to the right, the next road we take suddenly makes me feel like I'm heading into the rural part of Ohio. The houses are spaced acres apart as opposed to being right on top of each other. Growing up right on the lake, it can be easy to forget farmland takes up so much of the state. Fields and fields of agriculture and cows. So many cows.

"Hi moo moos!" Rose shouts as we pass a pasture full of them.

Burnham Orchards sits off a state road. At the very front of the farm is a market featuring local items and home-made goods from "Grandma Bea's Bakery." Rose and I both agree we'll stop there on our way out so we can try the homemade apple cider donuts. Once I park the car, I reach in the back seat for the two cute baskets Riley lent us to collect our apples. I had invited her to come, but she said she needed a day at home to be lazy and eat lots of chocolate which is such a mood that I couldn't argue.

The basket I hand Rose is all brown except for the red handle and top band. My basket is a light brown and has mixed blues and yellows all throughout the weaving. As we walk into the orchards, excitement courses through my veins and I feel like a little girl again as we prepare to pick our very own apples from the trees.

Our methods for picking apples are very different. Like a kid in a candy store, Rose pulls whatever apples catch her eye haphazardly. I take my time making sure each apple is a decent size and is free from blemishes. It doesn't take long for Rose to fill her basket to the brim and then join me to hurry my slow critiquing.

"It looks great to me!" Rose says as I scrutinize a low hanging fruit.

"I don't know," I turn it. "I wish it was a bit bigger."

"Picky are we?" Rose chuckles.

The same conversation happens two more times before I find another I'm willing to place carefully in my basket.

"So what else do you do for fun?" Rose asks when my basket is about three quarters full. "I'm curious to see if things have changed since I was young, wild, and free."

"Mostly hang out with my best friend Riley, cuddle with my cat, and read," I say. "I try to go for walks when the weather's nice, but I'm not always as good about that. Photography is something I've thought about getting into but haven't been brave enough to try yet. I am dating a guy named Sebastian right now."

"Ooh, very interesting," she giggles like a schoolgirl, "Tell me about him."

"He's nice," I pull another apple down after carefully examining it.

"That's it?" Rose switches which arm is carrying her basket. "How long have you two been dating?"

"Just a few weeks," I walk up to another tree. "He really is nice. The dates have been fun, and he's a good guy, I think."

"But he's a bad kisser?"

"No!" I turn to Rose as she picks up and surveys some apples in her basket. "He's not a bad kisser per se. The kissing is just...okay. I guess I don't feel a spark like I thought I would. But you think that means I should end things with him."

"Not necessarily," she shakes her head. "Hearing the details changes my opinion on that matter a bit but life is short and you should enjoy whoever you're spending your time with. If the rest of it makes up for the so-so kissing, then I think that's wonderful. I'm sorry for my extreme reaction when you asked before. I had some unpleasant experiences in the past."

"Oh?" I focus on the bright red apple I'm thinking about pulling down, not wanting to pry.

"My husband was an ass," she states plainly. "Malcolm treated me like a servant and when I didn't do what he wanted or had 'an attitude' about it, he'd slap me around. When we first started dating, he was sweet but once we got married everything was different."

"Rose, I'm so sorry."

She waves my concern away and says, "It was a long time ago. He died in a freak accident at the factory twelve years into the marriage when my youngest was only two. Left me to raise my babies by myself. It was tough but I think I did a good job."

"I can tell you're a wonderful mother Rose," I say to her. "Still, I'm sorry you had to go through that."

"My biggest regret is a man named Mateo," she says after a few beats of silence. "I met him while I was still married to Malcolm. To this day I'm certain he was the love of my life. He lived down the street and took his daughter to the same park I took my kids to. They'd play together, and we'd sit there and talk. He was so kind and sweet and made me feel seen. As a whole person, with thoughts and feelings and not just 'wife' and 'mother.' Nothing ever happened because I was too terrified of Malcolm but I always wonder 'what if.' Mateo moved to Seattle shortly before my husband died and I haven't seen or spoke to him since."

"Wow," is the only thing I can say.

Poor Rose. Abused for over a decade and then left alone with three young children. Possibly finding love and then losing it. She must be a force to be reckoned with to go through all that and still come out a fun and kind person who you'd never know went through such difficulties.

"Don't look like that," Rose scolds.

"Like what?"

"Like I'm something to pity," she thrusts out her chin. "Everybody's got pain and regrets. I found my strength and I'm proud of the life I've lived so far."

"As you should be," I tell her and mean it.

Rose is exactly the type of person I strive to be; resilient and tenacious. I make a vow that when I'm feeling down or frustrated with life, I'll remind myself to channel Rose and make good things happen.

It's so sad she had a chance at love and didn't get to make it a reality. Did Mateo feel the same way as Rose? It would be so cool if it could be like that movie *Letters to Juliet* and somehow Rose and Mateo find each other again after decades apart. The idea hits me and I can't contain my excitement and accidentally pull an apple from a tree as I spin around to face her.

"Rose! Let's find him!"

"Find who?"

"Mateo! We can try to find him online. Maybe he has a Facebook or something."

"I don't know about that. It's been so many years since we last saw each other. He's most certainly already married or he could even be dead for all I know. I'm not sure it's such a great idea."

"Obviously it's up to you, but I think we could at least try to see what he's up to. We don't have to reach out to him if you don't want to."

"Let me think about it," Rose stares off into the distance lost in thought.

I hope I didn't terribly upset her. I shouldn't have opened my stupid mouth and ruined her lovely day. I won't say anything else.

Right as I find my last perfect apple, Rose's phone rings and she answers the FaceTime from her son.

"Hi gwandma!" two identical little girls shout when the call connects.

"Well, hello Miss Morgan and Mallory! I'm so happy to see you!"

Rose takes a seat on the ground at the base of an apple tree and appears happy as can be talking to her cute granddaughters. I gesture to Rose, indicating I'm heading up to the market and take both our baskets to pay for them. Wandering around the store first, I grab two jars of locally collected honey, mixed berry jam, and two perfectly golden apple cider donuts dusted with cinnamon. I pay for everything and wait for Rose near the front door.

"Say hello to my new friend Melody girls," Rose instructs as she wanders in.

Morgan and Mallory both wave to me and shout "hi" from the phone screen with toothy smiles. They're both adorable and I'm reminded Rose is alone now that all of her kids and grandkids have moved away. Well, she has an honorary granddaughter here now.

The twins tell me they're making apple pie with their mom tomorrow and that they super-duper miss their Grandma Rose.

"I miss you too sweets. I'll come visit you soon."

Rose's son briefly hops on the screen to say hi to his mom and he resembles a younger male version of Rose with his rosy cheeks and kind smile. Instead of white hair he has deep chestnut brown hair I imagine is pretty similar to what Rose's must have looked like when she was younger.

When the call ends, Rose stares into space while turning her phone over and over. I want to say something more about finding Mateo but I hold my tongue. It sounds easy to me but I can't imagine being in her shoes. He could be dead, married to someone else, or just not interested. If I were in Rose's position, I'd be more than terrified.

I snap a picture of Rose in front of the Burnham Orchard's sign with her basket of apples to send to her family. Her happiness blossoms again and is infectious at the prospect of making apple pies.

"You'll have to bring a pie to the library on Monday. Share with your coworkers," Rose suggests on our drive back to her house.

"I'm not sure Jamie deserves a piece of our amazing pie."

I'm only half joking.

As we go back the way we came, Rose regales me with stories of her three grandchildren and gushes with love and affection.

"Mary had Aiden when she was only twenty-two. She told me the father was a one-night stand, and she'd be raising him herself. I was so scared for her because I knew how hard it was. And I never even did it with a newborn. She's so strong though and she's done everything she possibly can for that boy. She's a wonderful mother. I helped a lot when he was a baby but they moved to Cincinnati when he was in middle school so she could take a great job. I go down there every couple of months and they visit often enough."

"I'd love to meet them. They all sound fantastic."

The stories continue once we're back at Rose's house and in the full swing of pie making. Photos of her family cover the walls and each has a story. I could listen to her talk all day because she's such an excellent storyteller. Each tale is funny, thoughtful, and so full of life.

We follow an old Chapman family recipe Rose claims goes back fifteen generations. She makes the dough completely from scratch, explaining each step of the way and letting me knead the dough. Rose trusts me to drape a layer of the dough along the bottom of the pan. She then cuts the next layer of dough in pieces so she can set a braided pattern on the top when we're ready. In a bowl, we combine the apples with the sugar, flour, cinnamon, nutmeg, and salt. Rose throws in her secret ingredient she refuses to tell me and then we finish it up.

Once the pie goes in the oven, I feel a tremendous sense of accomplishment even though Rose did most of the work. She and I start a second pie and I monitor the oven window to watch as the crust turns golden brown. The aroma of the fruits and pastry fill the air. Even though I was at an apple orchard earlier today, it's this scent that makes me certain autumn has begun.

We pull the first pie out of the oven and it's picture perfect. I can't wait to take a warm and juicy bite. Rose pulls out home-style vanilla ice cream out of the freezer and cuts us each a piece with one perfect scoop of ice cream.

"Oh, my goodness this is amazing!" I moan after taking my first bite.

"It's pretty good if I do say so myself," Rose chuckles.

I savor the first few bites and then devour the rest of it, unable to stop myself from scarfing it down. It's too good. We use the remaining apples to make a batch of homemade apple cider and I'm in heaven.

"Thank you so much for everything, Melody," Rose says as she finishes her plate a couple minutes after me. "It was all so lovely."

"It was my pleasure Rose. I had a great time. I'm so glad you've become my friend."

"Believe me, I'm the lucky one," Rose pats the top of my hands with a kind smile.

Rose packs up the extra pie for me to take to the library and surprises me with a copy of the family recipe.

"Promise you won't share it with anybody else," Rose winks as she slips the sheet of paper into my purse.

"On my honor," I hold up the Girl Scout promise with my fingers even though I haven't done it since I was twelve or thirteen.

I take the metal tin carrying the extra pie and hug her goodbye.

"I'm really glad I met you Rose," I tell her with one foot out the door. "If you need anything, let me know."

"Same goes for you Miss Melody," Rose smiles and waves goodbye to me from her doorway as I drive away.

Chapter 8: A Courageous Heart

"This is so friggin' good," Jackson says for the third time as he picks up another slice of apple pie. "Thank you so much Melody."

"I'm glad you like it!"

"If anyone is looking for me at the desk, tell them I'm 'occu-*pied!*'"

"Oh my goodness," I roll my eyes but still laugh at his terrible pun.

"What's this?" Jamie strolls into the room.

"Melody brought apple pie for everyone," Jackson says.

Jamie turns to me for permission and I tell him to "go ahead and have a piece."

"It's amazing," I say as he sets a piece on a plate, "I actually made it with Rose this weekend. We went apple picking."

"That sounds fun," Jamie comments as he takes a bite.

His eyes widen and gapes at me in surprise. "Wow. You weren't kidding."

I hate how much his approval makes my stomach flutter. "Rose did most of the work."

"Don't sell yourself short Melody," Jamie scolds in a sweet tone.

"You ready for the class today?" I ask him, changing the subject.

"Absolutely," he smiles and looks me dead in the eyes.

My world shifts, and for a split second, I forget everything.

There's no recollection of the heartbreak or pain. I don't think of the betrayal or the anger and I definitely don't want to hate him as much as I should. All I can think about is that damn smile. The smile that undoes every ounce of torment and replaces it with wanting and causes goosebumps to spread across the back of my neck and arms in a wave making me shiver with desire.

Thank goodness I wore long sleeves today.

Fuck.

"Okay. See you later," I practically run from the room.

Why does he make me feel this way? Especially after everything that's happened, it's completely insane something so meaningless can still give me literal shivers. I want to scream. Why can't I control my own feelings and reactions? Goddamn him.

I hurry to the information desk and camp myself in front of my computer. I do everything I can to ignore the part of me that wants to make him want me again. The little devil version of me is sitting on my shoulder saying, "maybe you could have some fun with him. Make him pay you back for how he hurt you with some touching and feeling and kissing."

I pause my hands from typing the email I was responding to. Why don't I feel this way about Sebastian? I definitely want to punch Jamie in the face but I also want to jump his bones. At best, I want to give Sebastian a super friendly hug. Can I really make it work with him when that's all I feel?

"Melody!" Rose says as she appears in the library's entrance.

Grace gives her a chiding expression from the circulation desk and she waves an apology before continuing to rush over to me.

"Hey Rose, is it time for the class already?"

"Almost, but I actually made a decision. I want to do it."

My brain is still foggy from my earlier thoughts so it takes me a moment to realize what she's talking about.

"You want to find Mateo?" I ask and stand straight up from my seat in excitement. "What changed your mind?"

"I was thinking about our conversation before, about how I wanted to find new hobbies because I'm not getting younger, and the same applies in this situation. We may not find him or he may have no interest in hearing from me but why not try? At the very least, maybe I'll be reconnecting with an old friend. Either way, I've got a lot of life left to live and I will not waste it on regrets and what if's."

"That's incredible, Rose. If you want to stay after class today, we can start looking."

"Perfect. Oh, I'm so nervous and excited at the same time."

We both head into the meeting room where Jamie already has the computers set up. He's sitting on his own laptop at the front of the room appearing like he's doing some serious work when he catches us walking in.

"Hello ladies," Jamie gives us that smile and I remind myself once again I don't like him. "Rose, the pie you and Mel made was delicious. Thank you for sharing it with us."

"I'm so glad you enjoyed it," Rose gives me a knowing look, pleased I didn't withhold pie from Jamie.

"Usually I'd say pumpkin is my favorite fall pie but you might have made me a convert," Jamie chuckles and stands.

"Melody did most of the work," Rose straight up lies and Jamie holds in a laugh considering I said the exact opposite only a little while ago.

I talk about what we're going over in the program today so we can move on from the pie topic. The other seniors pile in and settle at the computers. I think we scared the group after last week's session on internet safety. Hopefully, we prepared them enough to learn properly how to search for things online and not accidentally give a fake foreign prince thousands of dollars.

All the seniors know about google and other search engines, but they find using it scary and overwhelming, which I don't blame them. There's so much information readily available, but it's all about how to decipher it into something usable and not accidentally click on a link that will corrupt your computer with spam and malware.

We do a few practice searches and I explain the different options that might pop up when you search for something.

"How do I know if it's the right thing I'm looking for?" Roberta asks.

"You go over all the information it gives you and determine if that matches what you're looking for."

Jamie pulls up google on the screen mirroring his laptop and searches for Walmart.

"If you click on the list that pops up, it will show you the different locations nearby and gives you their address and phone number. It will also give you the link to their website so you can go on there to make sure if it's legitimate in case you're on the hunt for something more obscure than Walmart."

The group collectively nods their heads but I'm fairly certain we'll be going over the same thing a couple more times. Especially during our last session when we give individual help. Rose and Robert appear the most confident while the rest of them seem wary but willing. I show a few more examples and Jamie and I both answer more specific questions until the hour is up.

As the seniors file out, they talk amongst themselves. I hear several of them discussing how different things are in today's day and age. Rose is sitting still in her seat but wringing her hands together while staring at the Google search page as she waits for me.

"Was there something else you needed Rose," Jamie asks as I say goodbye to Julietta and Santiago.

"Melody's going to help me with something before I head out," she says.

"Gotcha," he smiles and closes his laptop. "Let me know if there's anything I can do."

"Well, actually," Rose begins and I rush the couple out the door recognizing the twinkle in her eye. "It couldn't hurt to have extra brain power if you wouldn't mind."

"Not a problem."

"That's not necessary."

We both speak at the same time and glance at each other.

Shit.

"Thank you Jamie," Rose gestures for him to come sit on her left and I sulk over to sit on her right.

I one hundred percent didn't notice Jamie smells like the woods on a sunny day. Or that his royal blue button-up shirt was *just* tight enough to show off his abs and muscled arms causing his veins to pop out.

Nope. Didn't notice at all.

"So what do you need help with Rose?"

Rose tells Jamie she's trying to find Mateo and gives him a shorter version of their backstory, leaving out the stuff about her husband.

"He moved to Seattle so long ago," Rose tells Jamie.

"It will be easier to find him if you have more information," I say to Rose. "Do you remember anything else about him?"

"Well, his daughter's name is Isabella. I remember he was born in December because our birthdays were only a few days apart. I think he was only a year older than me, so born in 1953? Oh! His middle name is Gabriel. I remember thinking his full name was so beautiful to say, Mateo Gabriel Hernandez."

"That's a good start," I tell her and start searching.

I begin with google hoping to get lucky but there are too many results popping up. I include some of the information Rose gave me and it narrows the possibilities. What makes the search easier is his daughter's name. We could find two possibilities of Mateo Gabriel Hernandez's in the U.S., around the right age, with a daughter named Isabella. One is in San Antonio, Texas and the other is in Chicago, Illinois. However, there are no pictures and nothing else to help us decide which one could be the right one.

"What if neither of them are him?" Rose asks while chewing on her fingernails.

"They both had email addresses listed," Jamie reassures her. "We can email both and hopefully they'll respond."

Rose uses the skills we've taught her over the last couple of weeks to reach out to both of her potential suitors.

Dear Mateo,

My name is Rose Chapman. I'm not sure if you are the Mateo I'm looking for but I hope you are. We were friends a very long time ago in Lorain, Ohio when we used to take our children to the same neighborhood park. I understand you may not remember me, and in that case I apologize for bothering you. I know we haven't spoken in years, but I still consider you a very close friend and I was hoping to reconnect. If you are the Mateo I'm searching for, send me the name of the park where we met and hopefully we can become friends again in our old age.

Sincerely,
Rose Chapman

Rose hesitates over the "Send" button on the first email and she looks at me with indecision clear in her eyes.

"You can do this," I whisper and squeeze her free hand.

Without another thought, she clicks the mouse and sends the first email. Sending the second is even easier and then we're done. Rose shuffles about with huffs and puffs after, questioning whether it was the right decision. In the end, she packs herself up and heads home. I had helped access her email on her laptop at home in between pies this past weekend, so I imagine she'll be checking it all night long. I can't help but worry even if one of these Mateos is the right one, his computer skills will be lacking and he may not see this message for a long time, if ever.

Oh well. Nothing we can do but hope, wait, and keep our fingers crossed.

"I think it's cool how much you've been helping Rose," Jamie comments.

Lost in my own thoughts, I had forgotten he was still there.

"I don't see it as helping. I enjoy spending time with her like I would with any friend."

"Still, most people would be hesitant to befriend a senior. I like her a lot too. You can tell she's got a good heart."

"Yeah," I turn my focus to the wrinkles in my knuckle. "I feel guilty for suggesting this whole thing. I'm not sure I fully thought it through. He may not even respond and I don't want her to get hurt."

"The world can be a really shitty place. Finding happiness is worth it at any age. Happiness is a continuous quest, not a finite destination. We all find little joys along the way. If this path doesn't lead to joy, I'm sure she'll find another"

"Damn Jamie," I peer at him with my eyes wide. "Did you change your major to philosophy after we broke up?"

"Just the minor."

"Really?"

"No," his hand lands on his stomach and he gives me a deep chuckle. "Just experienced plenty of my own shit that I've been working on getting through."

I nod my head and force myself not to prod. I decide now is a good time to leave the room, happy to leave a conversation with Jamie on a relatively positive note.

"Thanks for your help Jamie."

"Anytime Mel."

"Melody!" Rose yells as she appears in the library's doorway for the second time in as many days.

By the look on her face, I already know what's coming.

"He responded?" I hurry to the other side of the desk to meet her halfway.

"I was about to go to bed when I saw the notification pop up. I couldn't believe it. Spent ten minutes staring at the darn thing before I got the courage to actually open it. I was certain it would be from one of them saying they weren't the right Mateo but it was him! He said he remembered me instantly, and that he was so happy I reached out."

"It was meant to be!" I clap.

Jamie pops his head out of his office at the commotion and I call out, "we found him!"

He rushes from the room to find out more.

"You're sure it was him? Did he remember the name of the park?" Jamie asks when he reaches us.

"He did! We even figured out how to start the chat feature in our accounts and we talked all night. He was the one living in Chicago. Apparently he got a job there after his daughter went to college and he's been there ever since."

"Where at? Melody and I both know the area."

"Some place called Oak Park?"

"Oak Park is awesome," Jamie and I both say at the same time.

"It's so sad. Apparently he broke his leg recently," Rose comments. "He was riding his bike when a car took a turn too fast and almost hit him."

"That's terrible," I say.

"Isn't it? That's why I thought it was a good idea for me to go visit him."

"What?" I'm taken aback figuratively and literally. "Are you sure?"

"I'm positive. He said he'd come here but he can't travel with his leg. Will you come with me Melody?"

I think about it for about two seconds. My first instinct is to say no and caution her against the whole idea, but I see young Rose peeking out from behind her eyes. She's hopeful and excited about something new and potentially wonderful and all she needs is a little help to get her closer to finding her joy. How could I say no?

"Of course, Rose. When do you want to go?"

"You know," Jamie interjects, "I'm actually going to Chicago this weekend to spend some time with my family since we have Monday off for Indigenous People's Day. I'd be more than happy to drive if you two want to join. Make it a fun road trip?"

You have got to be kidding me. This can't be happening. This is what I get for being nice. The idea of becoming an old hag who lives in the woods and scares people off with a broomstick and weird smelling concoctions becomes more appealing instantly.

"Oh Jamie, how perfect. It must be fate!"

Rose echoes my earlier words and I hold in a groan. There's no way I can do this. I've already agreed to go with Rose and I know she needs my support, but stuck in a car for over ten hours there and back with Jamie? There's no way. No fucking way. Jamie and Rose both look at me expectantly and my brain analyzes the situation as quickly as possible.

Rose's expression is so hopeful and pleading with me while his is unreadable. Does he really want me to go? He probably only offered out of fondness for Rose but I'm sure he's dreading it too. His thoughts are probably running like, *"Gee it sure would be nice to help Rose. It's too bad we have to drag my pathetic ex-girlfriend along. Hopefully she won't be more awkward and weird than usual."*

I wish I could text Riley. What would she say?

I know it'll be awkward but I'm sure it'll be completely uneventful Mel. It's two people in a car. So what?

So what? So uncomfortable. I have nothing to talk to him about and we can't not talk the whole time. What if we end up talking about us? What if he asks about Sebastian? What if we fight again? What if it's just weird?

You know how I feel about what if's. This isn't about you Mel. It's about Rose.

Shit.

"Sounds good to me," I say to them both about thirty seconds later than I should have.

"Thank you so much you two. I can't tell you how much this means to me."

"I'll plan on picking you both up first thing Saturday morning."

"Perfect," Rose says.

"Okay," I say.

Rose makes a sound I can only compare to a young girl's squeal and then waves to us both as she heads out of the library.

"I know this is a bit of a weird situation but how about we make a deal?" Jamie says.

"What's that?" I turn to him and bite my lip.

"Let's just pretend we never knew each other before starting this job. Pretend we're two new coworkers helping a mutual friend out and having an amicable road trip."

"I think we can make that work," I grin at him and am at least a little hopeful we can do this without it being intensely awkward.

I'm definitely not excited to be close to Jamie for three whole days. Not even a little bit.

"Liar."

Damn that little devil on my shoulder.

Chapter 9: A Disappointing Turn

The night before I leave to go on a road trip with my ex-boyfriend and new 65-year-old friend, I have a date with Sebastian. Talk about sentences I never thought I'd say. I'd never admit it out loud, but I'm more excited for the road trip than the date. It's not that I'm *not* excited for the date. The way Jamie makes me feel and the idea of being near him for such a long period of time makes me nervous and excited even though I know I shouldn't be.

I'm also pretty certain Sebastian's going to make a stronger move tonight to have sex and I haven't decided how I'm going to respond to it. On the one hand. Yay sex! On the other hand, it could be not awesome sex. The uncertainty of it makes me lean toward saying no but is that a good enough reason? It is just sex after all. I'm sure it won't be bad. Maybe it will be just as meh as kissing him.

I sigh so deeply my breath blows the fur on Lucy's back and she arches her back in annoyance. She stands, spins in a circle, licks the spot where I blew, and then sits back down giving me her gracious permission to continue petting her.

"Oh thank you, your majesty," I scratch her head and her purrs get louder.

I keep thinking the same things over and over while I pet and play with Lucy for twenty minutes. She distracts me long enough that soon I'm running late and I have to rush to get ready.

I hit play on my *Be a Badass and Powerful Woman* playlist which features a lot of Paramore, Halsey, and Chvches. My body is more like a tornado as I rush through picking out my outfit and redo my hair three times until I feel good about leaving it be. When my hair is in a perfect ponytail and I'm wearing tight jeans with a fitted blouse, cool jacket, and boots I feel at my most put together. Thank god my matching bra and panties made it through the wash. It's better to be prepared.

As soon as the clock strikes seven thirty, there's a knock on the door.

I open it and invite Sebastian in. He immediately gives Lucy a wary look and she mirrors it and walks into the other room. That's not a good sign. Sebastian's attention returns to me and he gives me a wide grin that gives me a shiver and I'm hopeful all my worries and fears amount to nothing at all.

"You look fantastic Melody," he says while flattening his gray long sleeve button-up.

"So do you," I attempt to flutter my eyes and tuck my hair behind my ear but I'm not sure if I pull it off or if I seem like I'm having some kind of spasm.

He leans down for a kiss and he lingers long enough for me to think, "okay that's good enough." Which is, objectively, probably not a good thing to think about the guy you're in the middle of kissing. When he pulls away, I give a coy smile. He sweeps his arm towards the door and says, "shall we, m'lady?"

I try to hide my cringe with an attempt at a flirty chuckle and walk out the door, making sure I turn the lock when I pass through. He follows and shuts the door behind him and I meet him at his car. He had told me he wanted the night to be a surprise so I'm hoping I dressed appropriately for wherever he's taking me.

He drives into Avon and we end up at a local place called Strip Steakhouse and as soon as we pull into the parking lot I've realized I've made a big mistake letting him surprise me because I do not like steak. At all. When I go to steakhouses, I usually end up getting chicken or a cheeseburger and whoever I'm with questions my sanity because how on earth could I not want a steak at a steakhouse? It's also a toss-up if a steakhouse can actually cook things other than steak well.

When we get to our table, Sebastian hits me with, "I called ahead and ordered the special dinner for two and their best wine."

"Oh!" Is all I can think to respond when I realize the dinner for two includes two six oz filets.

I scan the two pages of the menu to get an idea of what else they offer and the dollar signs next to each dish make my eyes bug out of my head.

"Sebastian, this is so sweet, but this place is too much. We didn't have to go somewhere so fancy."

"I wanted tonight to be special," he gazes up at me from under his eyelashes with his own version of a coy smile and my suspicions about sex being on the menu for tonight are confirmed.

"Of course," I try to smile back and immediately feel so guilty I don't like steak and that he's clearly very excited for the dish he wants me to serve later tonight.

It's not like steak makes me gag and throw up. I just never have a taste for it and it does nothing special for me. Every time I scroll by a video of some internet "influencer" cooking up their version of the perfect steak they eat the thing like it's the holy grail of food, weird throaty moan and all. Every time I've had steak, I end up shrugging and saying, "eh it's fine."

I can pretend to love it once. No big deal. Maybe this steak will surprise me and be better?

Little devil me on my shoulder has to insert herself into my personal thoughts with, "Isn't that what you keep saying about your kisses with Sebastian? How's that going?"

When the wine comes, Sebastian swirls the glass and sniffs it like some kind of wine connoisseur and tells me, "It's the perfect red to go with steak. Full-bodied and smooth."

"I'm sure you're right. My wine knowledge is more limited to the wine box section at the liquor store."

He appears slightly offended about my wine tastes but resets his face into his flirty grin. I'm frankly surprised a self-proclaimed sports guy is interested in wine. Maybe he's trying to seem sophisticated to impress me.

The meal arrives and I'm way more excited about the side salad and garlic mashed potatoes than I am the steak. When the server sets the meal in front of us, Sebastian looks so excited. He even rubs his hands together like he's preparing to devour the best meal he's ever had.

He gestures to me to take the first bite of steak and watches me closely. I can feel my face flush from his close attention and I channel every ounce of actress in me. Admittedly, it amounts to me playing a flower waving in the wind in my second-grade class play but damn did I play a convincing flower.

"Mmm, it's amazing!" I fib.

I can tell he's pleased by my answer and dives into his own plate. As I chew, it's obvious the steak is delicious but for my tastes, it's only okay. I take a few more obligatory bites, doing my best to convince him I'm loving every bite. Then I turn to my salad and demolish that. When I take my first bite of the mashed potatoes, I almost make the weird food moan because they are so damn good. Now potatoes are a food I'll happily eat all the time and gush about.

"I've just got to say," Sebastian interjects my third bite of mashed potatoes, "I've been looking for so long for a girl to call mine and I'm just so happy I met you Melody."

"Oh," I set my fork down, "that's so sweet Sebastian. I'm happy I met you too."

A girl to call mine? That's an odd choice of phrase. Old-fashioned at the very least. Oh well, it *is* sweet of him to say and I know he's trying to be romantic. I can only hope he doesn't become super co-dependent. I love being by myself far too much for that.

The sharing continues with our dessert, a double chocolate cake with a raspberry drizzle topped with vanilla ice cream. I've never had occasion to use the word delectable to describe something, but that time has come. The cake is rich and fluffy and combined with the slightly tart fruit flavor, my mouth tingles with each morsel. I saw on the menu the home-style vanilla ice cream is handmade on site and boy is it smooth, light, and creamy. The chef made it to perfection and I wish it had been my entire meal and not a split dessert with Sebastian.

"Wow, that's good," Sebastian comments.

"I know," I finish my half too quickly.

I keep hoping he'll offer the rest to me but he doesn't. I'll have to come back here on my own to get the mashed potatoes and this dessert again.

"Thank you for dinner," I follow Sebastian back to his car when we finish eating and he pays the outrageous check.

"Of course, Melody. It was my pleasure. So," he opens the door for me, "your place or mine?"

I have five seconds to answer before he climbs into the driver's seat. On the one hand, I've never had someone in my apartment to sleep with and it feels a little weird. On the other hand, I don't have my car so if I change my mind and want to leave, I would be stuck.

"Let's head to mine," I decide.

"You got it," he smiles and rushes out of the parking lot.

I wonder what he's excited for. God, now even my thoughts are sarcastic.

Lucy is already hiding by the time we get inside. I'm fidgeting with my clothes and hair and immediately start tidying up. I'm nervous because it's been awhile right? Right. Deep breaths Mel. Sex is awesome. Nothing to get worked up about.

"Why don't you come sit next to me? Sebastian pats the couch cushion and I make my way over.

"I'm a little nervous," he admits once I'm settled next to him.

"What are you nervous about?"

"I like you so much Melody and I want this to be incredible."

"I do too."

I smile and grip the couch cushion tighter. He slowly brings his lips to mine for an unfortunately boring kiss and my hopes for this night to be amazing are brought back to the level of it'd be nice if it was more than average. He makes his moves and we end up on my bed to do the deed.

It's nice to know the universe is at a place where consistency is key because my hopes are left wanting when the entire night is completely average. Sebastian is sweet and considerate the whole time but there just wasn't any spark. For me at least. No moment came where I found myself completely lost to the sensations and feeling like I don't want it to end because it feels so goddamn good. It was fine. Which seems to be the theme of all the time I spend with Sebastian.

"That was amazing Melody," Sebastian nuzzles his face into my neck.

"It was really great Sebastian," I hold the blanket in my hands making sure I cover my body, suddenly feeling self-conscious.

"I'm so glad," He kisses my neck and I immediately know I need to get him out of here or else he might want to stay the night and knowing my luck try again in the morning.

"Melody," he asks, "will you do me the honor of officially being my girlfriend?"

Awkward. Shit. Would I be truly terrible for saying no to that right after we have sex? Probably. I haven't officially made up my mind about how I feel about him or us so is it awful if I say yes with a caveat of *for now* in my head until I am sure? Also probably.

"Yes," I smile at him and kiss his shoulder so I can stop looking him in the eyes.

He puts his finger under my chin to move my face towards his and he kisses me in a way I'm sure to him feels like a boatload of passion.

After a few minutes, I pull away and tell him, "Hey, so I hate to kick you out but I've got an early morning tomorrow."

"I thought you didn't work tomorrow," his eyes find mine and I realize I hadn't mentioned my trip.

"I don't. I'm taking a bit of a spontaneous trip to Chicago with my friend Rose and my coworker Jamie."

"Why didn't you tell me?" His face grows darker with confused annoyance replaying his gleeful grin.

"I didn't think about it. It honestly just happened. I'm helping Rose reconnect with someone from a long time ago and Jamie was going to visit family so we're hitching a ride. I'll be back Monday night."

"Okay," he stands and starts getting dressed. "Well, I'll text you I guess. Remind me who Jamie is?"

"Oh, he's the IT guy at the library," I sit up and lean against my bed frame.

I'm pretty sure giving Sebastian the full background on Jamie would be a bad idea.

"He? I thought Jamie was a girl," Sebastian stops what he's doing and scrutinizes me.

"Oh...yeah, no he's a guy," I'm not sure what else to say.

"Okay," he finishes throwing his shirt on and then sits awkwardly on the bed. "How old is Jamie?"

"He's our age. Why?"

"I don't want you to forget about me," he says with a teasing voice but I can't help but think back to his earlier sentiment about me being his "girl to call mine" and wonder if he's jealous.

"You don't have to worry about that," I assure him.

"I better not," he has the same teasing tone as before but now it's partnered with a not so hidden undercurrent of a threat.

"I really do have to get up early so we can hit the road."

"I'll text you while you're on the road then," he kisses me and leaves.

I sit there for minutes after he leaves, trying to figure out how I feel. About Sebastian. About the sex. About my life. I don't come to any conclusions. There's only one thing I know I need to do before I can go to sleep.

I throw all of my sheets and blankets in the washer.

Chapter 10: Familiarity Breeds Contempt

My mug full of Darjeeling tea is piping hot and keeping my hands warm as I wait for Jamie to come pick me up. I had been petting Lucy but my continuous bouncing leg annoyed her enough she left my side in a huff and is now staring at me from the other side of the room. Probably wondering what the fuck is making me so agitated.

I'm not even sure I know the answer to that question. It would be easy to say it's the idea of spending so much time in the same car as Jamie but I don't think that's it. I don't want to admit, even to myself, it's because my attraction overshadows my animosity for him.

My phone rings and when I pick it up, I don't even get a hello in before I hear, "Stop freaking out so much."

"I'm not Riley," I bite back, annoyed for a moment she knows me so well.

"Yes, you are and we both know it. It's going to be fine."

The truth to my anxiety spills out because I'm unable to keep my feelings hidden from Riley. "Whenever I'm around him, I can't help remembering everything that happened and more than anything I'm embarrassed and ashamed. I can't stand the thought that I made such a fool of myself and he knows it, that he's probably thinking about how much of a freak I am every time he looks at me. And it doesn't help I'm still ridiculously attracted to him."

"Maybe you should tell him that."

"What? Why?"

"I don't know. To help clear the air? Make things less uncomfortable?"

I consider it for a moment, but the idea of having an open and honest conversation with Jamie sounds miserable. More than likely, I'll end up getting frustrated and saying something that upsets him and then we fight again. Not to mention 5 years ago, I was completely open and honest with him about my feelings and that got us in the situation we're in now.

"I don't think that's a good idea. Why don't we both pretend I'm completely fine and I'll fake it until I make it. Let's talk about your upcoming date with Jackson."

"You're killing me Mel."

"I know. Anyway, your turn."

"I'm nervous. We've been texting and I like him but this will be our first actual date since our schedules have been so conflicting."

"You'll have to keep me updated and if you need a bailout, text me 911 and I'll call pretending to be your mom having an emergency."

"But he knows your voice," she laughs.

"That's why I'll sound like this!" I say with my voice lower and more mature.

"Yeah, okay. I'm not sure that's as believable as you think it is," she cracks up. "Thanks for giving me a good laugh though."

There's a knock at the door and my head turns swiftly and then I stop moving entirely.

"Shit." My breathing gets faster and my leg moves even quicker than before.

"Whoa Mel. You've gotta breathe."

Riley says, "in, out, in out," slowly so I can follow along for five breath cycles.

"Okay, now go get the door. If you have to, have your headphones in the whole time or fall asleep. It'll be over before you know it."

"You better be right. Thanks Riley. You're the bestest friend ever, you know that right?"

"So are you. Love you."

"Love you too."

The line disconnects, and I take another deep breath before heading to the door. Once again I'm hit with a sight I'd never thought I'd witness, as Jamie stands at the door of my apartment. He's dressed in a fitted blue t-shirt and gray joggers with tennis shoes. Damn he looks good.

"Hey Mel," he greets me. "You ready to go?"

"Yeah, I just have to grab my stuff and say goodbye to Lucy. Come in for a second."

With permission given, he steps through the threshold and my nerves are running like electricity through my body.

"Lucy?"

"My cat. She was just here."

"Well hey there," I turn around to Lucy wrapping herself around Jamie's legs and arching her head up for scratches to which he abides.

"Wow. She rarely likes strangers."

"Lucky me. She's a sweetheart."

"When she wants to be." I give Lucy a dirty look, annoyed she's being so nice to Jamie when last night she snubbed Sebastian.

I grab my duffle bag out of the bedroom and walk one last time around the apartment to make sure I flipped all the lights off and my electronics are unplugged. I chug the last of my tea now that it's cooled off and set the mug in the sink.

"Alright, I'm ready," I walk back into the living room and now Lucy is comfortably curled up on Jamie's crossed legs.

"I'm not sure she's going to let me go," he chuckles.

"You're so spoiled Lucy," I go over to grab her and pause with my hands midair once I realize how close I'd be to touching Jamie's lap. "Um, you can just push her off. She'll be fine."

Jamie carefully wraps his hands around Lucy's torso near her front legs and moves her carefully off his legs. She looks peeved but when he sets her down she leaves without a fight. Jamie glances down at his lap and my eyes can't help but follow and I cover my mouth to contain my laughter.

"Sorry, hazard of living with a cat," Jamie brushes the gray hair off his lap.

For a split second, I consider reaching out to help but remember my earlier dilemma and leave him to it. Even after a few minutes of brushing the fur is still sticking to his pants and he gives up with a shrug.

I scoop Lucy up and give her a squeeze which results in a meow of complaint. I give her a smooch on her cute little forehead and rub her side. She pushes her head into my chin and I hear her purring which calms my earlier nerves. Part of me wishes I could take her with me but I'm certain she wouldn't like that as much as I would.

"I'll see you in a couple days Lucy. Riley will come check on you tomorrow."

"I've never known a cat to be so affectionate," Jamie comments after I lock the door and we head to his car.

"It's a common misconception that cats aren't affectionate. They just reserve their affections for those they like and have a connection with. They're not like dogs who give it up for anyone that walks on by."

"That's a harsh view of dogs. Do they honestly deserve that?"

"Maybe not, but what can I say? I'm a cat person."

You would think I'd have noticed Jamie's car by now, but it's escaped my notice he has a very nice-looking Jeep Cherokee. I wonder what he must have been doing for work before he came to the library and if it paid better. If so, why would he leave there to work here?

He opens the trunk and offers his hand out for my bag which I give to him and he tosses it in. We both climb in the front seats and I give him directions to Rose's house. In between, "turn here" and "it's straight for a while" we exchange niceties but our conversation doesn't get deep. When we reach Rose's house, she's already standing outside with her bag and positively bouncing with excitement.

Jamie climbs out to throw her bag in the trunk and help her into the backseat. Once she's settled and Jamie's in the driver's seat again he asks, "are we ready."

"Yup," I nod.

"Absolutely," Rose confirms from the back.

"On we go," Jamie sets the directions on his phone to display on the screen and we make our way.

"So how was your date last night Melody?" Rose asks out of nowhere.

I turn in my seat to give her a grimace and she appears guilty and mischievous at the same time. I'd mentioned it to her the other day. Facing the front again, Jamie's eyebrows raise higher, but he says nothing.

"It was great. He took me out to dinner at a pretty fancy steakhouse."

"But you don't like steak," Jamie says and I blink a few times.

How on Earth does he remember that?

"He wanted to surprise me and that tidbit about myself hadn't come up yet. I still enjoyed the meal."

"What did you order?" Rose asked. "I love steakhouses."

"Well," I hesitate to answer, "part of the surprise was that Sebastian called ahead to order the special steak dinner for two."

"He ordered for you?" Jamie sneers.

"He was trying to be romantic. It was really nice of him. The food was super good."

"But you didn't like it," Jamie stated matter-of-factly.

"It's the thought that counts," I reiterate.

Jamie says nothing else but his face relates enough about what he thinks about Sebastian. I want to tell him he can shove his opinions but I keep it to myself. My phone vibrates in my pocket and there's a text from Sebastian hoping I have a good day of driving with another not-so-subtle reminder not to "forget him." Great.

I decide to move the conversation from me and ask, "Is your family doing anything special this weekend Jamie?"

"Yeah, we're having a bit of a get together," he responds vaguely.

"Like a reunion?" Rose probes.

"Something like that," Jamie responds without more detail.

After a few comments about not sleeping very well the night before because she was nervous, Rose passes out in the back seat and Jamie and I sit in silence for a bit before he asks me if it's okay to put on some music.

"Promise anything but Florence and the Machine," I plead.

"I've never understood your issue with them. They're great," Jamie shakes his head.

"She screeches through most of her songs."

"That's so mean!"

"Is it mean or is it true?"

"They aren't mutually exclusive Mel."

"So you admit it!"

"I admit nothing. I think they're a great band."

"To each their own," I say as he turns on his music.

As soon as he hits shuffle on his playlist, the first thing that comes up is "The Dog Days Are Over" and I burst out laughing. I hear Rose stir in the back seat and I quiet my laughter a little. Jamie gives me a look but skips the song. I'm a lot happier when Paramore comes on.

We both listen to the music comfortably for a while. I watch out the window as we drive west on the turnpike. We're on this road for such a long time and there's not much to pay attention to besides the other cars and their passengers.

"You've got to be kidding me," I comment as a blue Volvo passes. "This guy's picking his nose! Why do people seem to forget most car windows are still see-through?"

"Ew," Jamie laughs. "I just saw another guy rocking out to what I assume was a hair band given the way he was banging his head."

"That sounds dangerous," I crack up with him.

I peek at Jamie while he's laughing, and my heart softens a little. Right now he looks so sweet I can almost forget. And sexy. He has his hand thrown up on the wheel casually showing off the muscles in his arm and his lean body sits straight in the seat. If this were a different time, I'd reach my arm over and rest my hand on his thigh and rub it with my thumb.

Stop it Melody.

A memory pops up of him shirtless and I feel my whole body flushing, my stomach filling with butterflies as the memory becomes one of a less family friendly nature.

Shit.

I shouldn't be thinking about this. Jesus, I had sex with Sebastian last night. Why am I not thinking about that? Why am I getting more excited thinking about a guy I last had sex with five years ago than the one I was with less than twelve hours ago? Am I terrible? I'm terrible. Ugh. I should have been smart and stayed away from all guys. Be celibate.

"What are you thinking so hard about?" Jamie interrupts my thoughts.

Awkward.

"Oh nothing," I turn my head to the window so he can't see the blush overtaking my entire face.

A question I had earlier pops back into my head and my curiosity wins out over prudence.

"Why did you move away from Chicago Jamie? I thought you loved it there."

His mouth forms a straight line and I'm immediately certain I've asked a question I shouldn't have.

"I'm sorry, you don't have to answer if it's too personal. It's none of my business."

"It's not that," he hesitates before reluctantly continuing. "My grandfather died."

"Oh Jamie," I cover my mouth with my hand. "I'm so sorry."

"Thank you," he gives me a soft smile before focusing on the road. "I had already been dealing with some shit and then in March he had a stroke and didn't make it. It just forced me to confront a lot, and it made me realize I needed a change."

"I can't even imagine," I say. "I remember how close you said you were."

"We had his funeral back in March but his birthday is this weekend so we're having a small get together to celebrate his life."

"I think that's sweet," I don't know what else to say.

"To be honest, I'm not looking forward to it," he takes a deep breath. "The funeral was hard enough. Am I supposed to pretend to be happy now while talking about my dead grandfather"

Now I'm really at a loss. I try to think of what I might say to comfort him and am reluctant to say anything in fear of saying something wrong.

"If it's a celebration of his life, that's what you need to do. Think of your favorite moments with him. The memories that give you the most joy so you can share them and preserve them. Death is an ending for one but a beginning for everybody else. The best thing you can do is find a way forward in a way that feels genuine and right for you."

He doesn't respond at first and I'm worried I said something to upset him but then he nods and says, "thank you Mel. That was helpful."

"Of course."

We both sit in reflective silence, save the music playing through the speakers. Every once in a while I hear soft snores drifting up front from the back seat and it makes me smile. Rose is the sweetest woman, and she deserves the world.

Even though I'm young, I've gotten to a place where I'm not as focused on finding happiness. It's been too easy to get hung up on when things go bad and being afraid they'll keep going bad that I've lost my appreciation for when things go right. Rose is teaching me life is about going after the things that bring you happiness. Wonder and amazement aren't only for the young, it's all a part of being human.

Sebastian texts three more times during the drive. I respond to the first two with short answers but am so annoyed with him texting me I turn my phone off. I'll call him tonight and tell him it died.

I keep catching glimpses of Jamie out of the corner of my eye and I both love and hate it. Alright, I've got to allow myself something. There's nothing wrong with looking at him and appreciating his fine form. He broke my heart not my eyes. There's no use in feeling ashamed over my attraction to him. I'm finding the joy in life right? His arms bring me lots of joy.

The hours pass by quicker than I thought they would and before I know it, we're crossing the border between Indiana and Illinois. There's not much difference other than there seems to be a ridiculous increase in the amount of billboards on the Illinois side of the turnpike. And the traffic is worse. I'd forgotten how terrible Illinois drivers are. They change lanes without signals. They go slow then out of nowhere start going eighty. Drivers in Illinois only care about themselves and getting where they're going as fast as their car can go.

I reach up to grab the handle above the window, worried our luck will run out and we'll get cut off by the wrong driver. Jamie's focus narrows in on the road ahead of him and he doesn't so much as flinch as he navigates the hell that is the highway into Chicago. Even as a native, he seems nervous to be driving these roads.

Rose perked up almost as soon as we entered the state but her expression morphed from excitement to nervousness with every mile. I don't think she's nervous for the same reasons I am. I can only imagine her thoughts as she readies herself to meet the man she was in love with decades ago.

The city comes into view and I'm filled with a sense of wonder. The Chicago skyline creates a magical feeling deep in my soul that makes me suddenly believe anything can happen. From the carefree zest for life in Wicker Park to the material opulence of the Gold Coast, and all the other distinct neighborhoods, there's so much to do and so many people to see. It's not hard to understand why people fall in love with this city.

We head into the heart of Chicago and it brings back so many memories of times when I'd explore on my own. The few memories I have of being in the city with Jamie skirt the edge of my mind but I push them away in favor of my own adventures. I notice Jamie peek over at me and I wonder what he's thinking about. He's got a lifetime of memories compared to my few years.

"Wow," Rose's glues her face to the window to take in the city as we drive in. "I've always wanted to visit Chicago but haven't been able to make it happen. It's so big."

"Chicago at dusk is my favorite," Jamie says. "The hustle of the day is winding down and the lights on the skyscrapers and other buildings are all coming on. There's something magical about the in-between time between day and night. You both see and feel the city transform in front of your eyes."

Rose and I are both stunned at Jamie. His words were poetic and I think we both were not expecting a guy known for his work in IT to speak in such beautiful prose.

Jamie glimpses at Rose in the rearview and then over to me before asking, "what?"

"Nothing. That was just...really lovely."

Jamie turns his head to the window so his expression is hidden but I can tell his mouth turns into a soft smile by the way the muscles on the side of his face move.

"Can we stop please?" Rose asks, panic entering her voice.

"Stop where?" Jamie and I both ask.

"Anywhere. I need a minute before we get there."

Once we get out of the city, Jamie pulls into a Starbucks. We follow Rose in, who heads straight to the bathroom. Jamie orders a vanilla latte and plops into the seat. I sit across from him but keep my eye on the bathroom door in case Rose needs anything.

After five minutes, I get worried and let Jamie know I'm going to check on her.

"Rose," I knock three times on the door. "Are you okay?"

She opens the door a crack and peers through.

"I'm not sure," her voice is softer than normal.

"Can I come in?"

She opens the door wider and waves me in. I turn sideways to squeeze in and say, "what's going on?"

"I'm nervous," Rose admits reluctantly while she runs her hands over her lavender blouse.

"Why?"

"Well," she sputters. "We've only been catching up on everything that's happened over the last few decades. We've had no talk of feelings or anything like that. Not to mention, I'm not as young as I was when he used to know me. What if he doesn't like what he sees?"

Since I met Rose, I've only known her to be a confident spitfire that makes her own way in the world. Seeing her so vulnerable and unsure of herself reminds me we're all more similar than we think. We all experience moments of fear and questioning along with joy and surety and that's a part of riding on life's tumultuous rollercoaster.

"Oh Rose," I give her the best, most comforting hug I can, "it's going to be okay. I know it is. Mateo wouldn't have responded if he didn't want to see you. Don't forget he's gotten older too and most certainly doesn't look like the man you knew all that time ago."

"I know. I can't possibly imagine him as anything but handsome."

"And if I had to guess, he won't see you as anything but beautiful."

"Oh goodness," she gives an uncertain smile and scrunches her nose, "I don't know about that."

"This isn't the Rose I know. What's really behind this?"

Rose washes her hands and waits until she's done holding them under the blow-dryer to respond.

"Back then, I was only a shell of myself. Ninety-five percent of my energy and strength went to protecting and taking care of my kids. What little I had left went to tiptoeing near Malcolm so he wouldn't slap me around. I'm so far from the same person I was and I don't know if Mateo will still see me the way he saw me back then."

"I'm sure, even back then, he saw the real you. Either he'll see you and love you now, or he won't. That doesn't diminish you. It allows you to accept things as they are and move on to the next amazing thing."

"I can't tell you how much I want it to be the former. I was so unbelievably head over heels for that man."

"Knowing you, I'm sure he was just as head over heels too. How could he not be?"

"You're the sweetest thing Melody. Thank you so much for helping this old lady."

"You're helping me just as much, Rose."

I leave so Rose can fix up her hair and makeup.

"All good?" Jamie asks when I sit back across from him.

"She's nervous but I think she's ready."

"I'll be able to drop you guys off and hang out briefly to make sure you're all good but I'll have to leave pretty quick to make it to my family's thing on time."

"That's fine. I plan on staying with them tonight and we'll take an Uber to our hotel later. If she feels comfortable, I'll take the train into the city tomorrow and spend the day so they can have some time alone."

"Be careful in the city by yourself," Jamie fixes his gaze on me with genuine concern in his eyes.

My first thought is how sweet it is for him to worry about me. My second thought is why couldn't he worry about my heart five years ago as much as he seems to be worried about me getting mugged.

"I'll be fine," I say with intentional coolness. "I used to go to the city all the time by myself."

I'm hit with the moments that came in the few months following our breakup and losing all my friends where I wasn't fine and I wasn't taking excellent care of myself. The memories rush through my mind on a loop and I feel my face flush and my stomach fill with anxiety.

"Are you alright?" Jamie asked.

"Yes," I study the smudges on the table, not wanting to reveal all of my emotions to him.

"I'm ready!" Rose pops out from the bathroom much perkier than before.

"Alright let's do this," I stand and head out the door in front of them both.

It only takes about five minutes to get to the address Mateo sent Rose. We pull up in front of a brown and white two-story Tudor-style house. It's not as big and luxurious as some houses in Oak Park, but it's a good size and looks comforting and cozy.

As we pull into Mateo's driveway, I catch Rose fidgeting with the hem of her shirt and tell her, "you can do this."

She nods firmly and quits fidgeting.

The car stops and we collectively take a deep breath before climbing out. Jamie and I stay back at the car so Rose can knock and say hello alone.

"I don't know why I'm so nervous for her," Jamie admits as she knocks on the door.

"We don't want her to get hurt."

An older Hispanic man with white hair and one large strip of gray answers the door with a huge smile. He's aged well and is quite handsome and Rose is practically vibrating as she reaches out her hand to re-introduce herself to the man she loved once upon a time.

"I think it's going to be okay," I say when Rose gestures for us to meet her at the door.

Chapter 11: A Second Chance

As we approach the door, Rose turns back to us and I'm certain she's probably only been happier when her children and grandchildren were born.

"Mateo, these are my new friends Melody and Jamie," we both shake his hand. "They were kind enough to escort me here."

"That's so nice of you," he greets us in a deep yet melodic voice. "I can't believe it's been so long. Rose looks exactly the same."

Rose blushes like a schoolgirl and shakes her head in denial before stating, "I'm sure that's not true but it is sweet. You don't look too different yourself. The white hair is a bit striking."

He runs his hand through his hair and that's when I notice he is indeed leaning on crutches and says, "I couldn't fight it."

Jamie glances over to me and subtly asks if he's good to leave with a nod of his head toward the car. I nod, feeling confident we're both safe with Mateo.

"It was very nice meeting you Mateo but I do have to go. Let me go grab your bags and I'll be back to pick you girls up on Monday."

"If you aren't going far, let me please invite you to dinner tomorrow night, as a thank you for helping Rose come visit me. I was thinking I could make the four of us my special enchilada recipe."

Jamie thanks him and tells us he can make that work. Rose gives him a hug and lets him know how much she appreciates him helping her and driving all the way here. My goodbye to Jamie is curt, and he raises his eyebrows but doesn't stick around to ask about it. When he brings our bags to the door, he waves once more and runs back to the car.

Mateo invites us in and we settle in the living room which is nicely styled with matching blue furniture. There's lots of pictures of a younger woman who I assume is his daughter. I wonder though if the room is so well styled because he maybe has a wife or girlfriend who's helped him decorate.

"Your home is beautiful," I comment before sitting on the loveseat.

"Thank you. To be honest, I'm hopeless at decorating but my daughter Isabella has become a wonderful interior designer and helped me spruce it up when I got the place."

The rest of the night, I feel entirely like a third wheel on a date. Rose and Mateo spend hours reminiscing about the old days and catching up on everything that's happened in between now and then. I add a comment here and there but their eyes and words are only for each other.

I'm about ready to interrupt their hour long discussion of their kids to recommend Rose and I leave for dinner when Mateo offers to take her out, just the two of them.

"I hope you don't mind," he comments politely. "I'll drive Rose to the hotel when we're done."

"Absolutely not," I smile and make arrangements for an Uber to come get me. "I hope you guys have an incredible time."

Rose is smitten when I wave goodbye from the car as she constantly keeps finding Mateo with her eyes. I'm so excited for her. This meeting couldn't have gone better. My evening is also going to be perfect as I put on my coziest pajamas, order a Chicago deep-dish pizza to devour, and watch my favorite rom coms.

The first movie begins, and I hit the power button on my phone and am greeted by two more texts from Sebastian "just checking in." I was going to call him but I decide I'm better off sending a message back. I let him know we made it okay and that I'm tired after a long day of traveling and I'll text him tomorrow.

Like magic, right when I finish *How to Lose a Guy in Ten Days*, Riley calls to check in on my sanity.

"It was amazing Ri. Rose and Mateo started acting like they'd seen each other yesterday and not decades ago. I'm not sure what is going to happen with them but I know it'll be good."

"That's really great. But how are you?"

"I'm perfectly fine. Jamie and I didn't even get in an argument the entire drive. We even had a moment where we were joking around. Maybe I'm finally learning to be comfortable around him again."

"Oh, yeah?"

Am I surprised she sounds so unconvinced? Not really. I thought I was pulling it off better though.

"Okay, I'm a little closer to maybe one day learning to be around him without wanting to scream."

"That's what I thought," she chuckles.

"It's fine. I won't even see him again until tomorrow at dinner and then maybe Rose can sit in the passenger seat on the way home."

"Maybe. What's your plan for tomorrow?"

"I'm planning on spending the day in the city. Giving Rose and Mateo some space. I thought I'd go to my favorite bookstores and get lunch in the city. Keep it low-key. Are you ready for your date?"

"I'm nervous," she admits. "I haven't been on a good date in a while. What if he's a terrible kisser like Sebastian?"

"Hey," I laugh a little, "I told you, it's not that he's bad, he's just meh."

"Still."

"I'm sure it'll be great Riley. You're amazing and he's super cool too. It'll be fun."

"Thanks Mel. I've got to go. He'll be here soon. Call me tomorrow and take lots of pictures of the city."

"I will. Love you."

"Love you too, best friend."

I hang up and start *You've Got Mail* and settle back into the mattress that feels like a cloud compared to my firm mattress at home. It's lovely for sitting and relaxing but it might be a little too soft for me to sleep on comfortably.

Rose floats into the room at nine thirty as if she's lighter than air.

"I'm guessing it went well?"

"It was wonderful Melody," Rose falls onto the other bed. "He was exactly as I remembered him. So sweet, caring, and kind."

"I'm so glad it's going well."

Rose sits up from the bed and stares at me directly before confessing, "He told me he fell in love with me all those years ago but knew I was married and that's why he never said or did anything!"

"You're kidding!" I sit up straight and throw my hands together, almost as though I'm praying. "Did you tell him how you felt?"

"I did! Somehow he still seemed astonished despite having just told me how he felt. The night was incredible. I'm ridiculously overjoyed."

"So what now?"

"I'm not sure. We talked about it a little but I think there's a lot more talking still to come."

"Well, you'll have the whole day tomorrow just the two of you to talk and figure it out."

"Are you sure? I feel terrible I made you come all this way for you to be all by yourself."

"Don't worry about me. There are a lot of bookstores I've been wanting to revisit and we'll meet up again for dinner."

"Lovely. Oh, I feel like a young woman again!" Rose squeals and falls back on the bed laughing and I do the same.

The next morning, Mateo picks Rose up at eight a.m. sharp and they go off to enjoy their time together. The Chicago Metra train stop is a short walk from the hotel and the routine for getting into the city is familiar. A short twenty-minute ride later, I arrive at Ogilvie Station and ready myself to be a temporary city girl.

My first stop is Sandmeyer's Bookstore, a twenty-five minute walk from Ogilvie. The inside is a mix of brick and industrial, which I've seen a lot of in Chicago but I still love it. I run my hands over the spines of the books, secretly wishing there's some magic tucked away in them that will transport me into a new and fantastical world.

No such luck. Oh well. Reading about the fantastical worlds is a close second.

I buy an on sale fantasy book and add it to my bookbag. From Sandmeyer's, I walk twenty minutes north to get to Barbara's

Bookstore which is a tiny but lovely shop. I wander around the store the same way I did in the previous and appreciate all the books and gifts for bibliophiles. Is there anything better?

In another life, I might have enjoyed working in or owning a small bookshop but I've come to terms with not having the fortitude to run a business or deal with the hectic frustrations of working retail. Still, I'll visit every independent bookstore I can and support them when I am able.

At Barabara's, I take home a small journal perfect to fit in my purse. The cover features a beautiful painting of what I imagine is an enchanted forest. I plan to fill the pages with to-do lists and random thoughts.

Sebastian texts twice while I'm exploring and his intrusions are getting on my nerves. I text him back but I keep my responses short and let him know after the second message I'm turning my phone off to preserve the battery. It's a lie but I need to be alone with my peace.

Sooner than I imagine, it's lunchtime, and I head fifteen minutes south by foot. Nestled right near the Chicago River is a little restaurant named Beat Kitchen on the Riverwalk. I order the Beat Salad with chicken and settle on the cement steps perfect for relaxing right by the water.

I was worried the pear, bleu cheese, and red onion would make an odd combination but somehow it works. I gobble the food down and feel refreshed and ready to take on the rest of the city.

"Melody?"

There's no fucking way.

Of course there is.

He's standing a few steps above me and looking like he was about to sit down but stopped when he noticed me below. He's got plastic ray-ban sunglasses on and is wearing deep blue washed jeans and a black shirt.

"Jamie? What are you doing here?"

Why does this keep happening? Getting a new job at the same place is a ridiculous coincidence but what are the chances of accidentally running into each other in a city of almost three million people?

"Uh," he walks down the steps and sits next to me, "I needed a break from my family."

"And you chose the Riverwalk?"

"I find people watching relaxing," he shrugs. "What are you doing here?"

"I'm about finished with lunch. I was going to head to another bookstore."

I'm pretty sure whatever mystical force keeps having him randomly appear everywhere I go also makes the next words come out of my mouth without my permission.

"Do you want to come with me?"

"Really?" He asks with eyebrows raised.

"Uh yeah," I take the last bite of my salad and shrug. "Why not?"

"Okay," he slaps his hands and his legs before standing. "Where to?"

"I was going to walk to After-words Bookstore then go relax at Navy Pier for a bit. It was always my favorite place to visit."

"Sounds good to me. God, I haven't been to Navy Pier since I was a kid."

"I've heard it's changed a lot over the years. You can play tourist for the day. Pretend you're somebody that's not a Chicago native."

"Hmm, I feel like I should be dressed in khakis and wearing a fanny pack to play tourist."

"I'm sure you won't stand out too much."

It only takes about ten minutes to walk to the bookstore. I know there's a ton of public transportation in the city including the L, but I prefer walking as long if there's time. I'd feel like I was missing out on things as I zoom by on the train. Plus, the exercise doesn't hurt. Well, it does hurt later but I've been informed it's "good for me" so...

Like Sandmeyer's, this shop is a mix of brick and industrial piping throughout the inside. All the stacks are tall and made of light wood. There's a ton of different displays curated with exciting selections from the staff.

"Did you guys need help today?" the young lady at the checkout counter asks soon after we walk in.

"No thanks, we're just browsing."

"Actually, I was hoping you could help me find something," Jamie walks up to the counter.

I walk away so I don't intrude on their conversation. I notice quickly that she is beautiful. Her long black hair is in dreadlocks, with the top section pulled up in a large bun. There are pretty blue beads set in each of the sections. Her makeup is as flawless as her warm brown skin and it's impossible not to notice she's super thin. When Jamie gets up to the desk, she leans forward with her chin resting on her palm. I wonder if the flirting is as obvious to Jamie as it is to me.

I watch Jamie from the corner of my eye to gauge whether he's interested at all in her attempts. He's smiling, and he's got his hand casually in his pocket. I think back to those few weeks right before we started dating. Did he act the same? I think he did. How could he not be flirting with her? She's gorgeous and works in a bookstore so she clearly has good taste.

Why do I care? He's not my boyfriend anymore. The surge of jealousy rises in me and my muscles tighten. The scrunch in my face and narrowing of my eyes is an uncontrollable response. I flee to the other side of the bookstore so I don't have to watch anymore.

It annoys me I had such a reaction. I have a boyfriend now. I think back to when he asked me to be his girlfriend right after we finished having sex. At the time, it felt like the right thing to do. Reflecting on it now though, it felt more of a heat of the moment *this is what is supposed to happen* yes than an *I have strong feelings for you and want to be in a relationship with you* yes.

When Jamie asked me to be his girlfriend all those years ago, it was an enthusiastic and instantaneous yes. I had been dreaming and hoping for the moment so when it finally came while we were lying in bed together in his dorm room; it was the easiest yes ever.

The moment was so similar with Sebastian but felt so different. Part of me wants to sit here and go around and around thinking of reasons that might be and why I should give Sebastian more time, but I'm sure of it now. I don't feel the way I want to about Sebastian. The way I used to feel about Jamie. Maybe I'll never feel that way about a guy again but that doesn't mean I should settle for less.

Despite the pain that came along with it, being with Jamie filled me with such happiness and such passion I can't imagine continuing to be with someone I don't even feel a fraction in comparison.

I've made my decision. I'm going to break up with Sebastian. We have plans to go to the harvest festival next weekend. Maybe I can meet him early and simply end it. Or maybe do it after the festival? I don't want to miss the event but what if he decides to still go too and then it's awkward? I'll have to ask Riley what she thinks.

"There you are," Jamie pops up from behind a stack of books.

"Here I am," I pull a book from the shelf and pretend I'm very interested in it.

"I didn't know you were an Occult enthusiast," Jamie teases.

I close the book and curse myself for not paying attention to where I was or what I was grabbing and then say, "it never hurts to expand your horizons."

"Just let me know if I should look out for a curse coming my way," he sounds like he's joking but his face looks like he might be a little scared.

"Now why would I have any reason to curse you Jamie?" I feign dumb.

"Maybe you really hate the way I type on the computer? I don't know," he wanders to the next aisle and I follow him.

When I turn the corner, I'm surprised to catch myself from completely running into him and our faces are millimeters apart when I stop myself. My breath catches and I can't move. We gaze into each other's eyes and the moment becomes frozen in time. His scent reminds me of a musky vanilla and it's intoxicating. I can hear him breathing and I suddenly want to reach my hand out and place it on his chest so I can feel the breaths as they go in and out. Move my hand down, down, down, and then-

"Sorry," I back away quickly and run into the shelf behind me, almost knocking a ton of books on the ground.

"No, I'm sorry," he catches the books I almost knock over and pushes them back on the shelf.

What the hell just happened?

"Did you find what you were looking for?" I hate that my voice is strained.

He's probably standing there thinking about what a freak I am.

"No, they didn't have it," I turn, and he's browsing the shelf not focusing on me.

"Gotcha," I turn away and pretend to be searching for something in my purse.

I walk away from him and back to the front of the store. I'm so confused. I've moved on from him, haven't I? Why is he affecting me this way? Maybe I should have meaningless sex with him. Get it out of my system. Of course, that would mean he would have to want to have meaningless sex with me which I highly doubt. I've got to keep my distance. This isn't healthy and awkward moments like that definitely aren't helping the situation.

At the front of the store, I find an old-fashioned looking fountain pen I decide will be my one purchase from this store. It's a perfect addition to my pen collection only Riley knows about. I started the collection a few years ago, and it has grown from a drawer full of pens I like to an eclectic collection of quirky and cool writing utensils.

I check out with flirty girl whose actual name is Delilah according to her name badge. God, even her name is pretty. I'm sure Jamie's actually thinking about having fun with her. He's probably hoping to find an excuse to move back to Chicago. I hope he does. It would save me a lot of trouble.

"Thank you again for your help," Jamie says to Delilah after he walks up behind me.

She side-eyes me and then looks back at him, her face settling into a subtle sneer and literally moving my stuff out of the way in dismissal to respond, "oh, I was more than happy to help. If you need anything else at all, please just let me know."

Okay chicky. Rein it in.

"Have a good day," Jamie dismisses her with noticeable coolness and walks away.

She and I both stand there watching him go, similar expressions of shock on our faces. She glares at me and I shrug and repeat Jamie's sentiment before following him out.

"We walking to Navy Pier?" Jamie asks out on the sidewalk.

"That was the plan," a strong breeze whips through and blows my hair all about.

By the time the wind dies, my hair closer resembles a puff ball and I groan as I run my hands through it trying to work out the knots.

"Thank you for reminding me why I don't like this city," I grumble to the sky.

"They don't call it the windy city for nothing," Jamie laughs and moves a piece of hair from in front of my face.

Is it just me or does he linger for a half second longer than he should?

I smile and glance down before grabbing my bookbag and digging for my hairbrush and hair band. I probably should have put it up in a ponytail from the get-go this morning but my hair was looking cute for once and I thought I'd enjoy it while it lasted.

"Alright, let's go."

If this were another time, Jamie and I might hold hands while we walked. Now though, our hands hover a short distance from each other, not touching but close enough to feel the air flowing between us.

We talk about little things as we walk. Mostly work. I mention Riley and Jackson and he's intrigued by the gossip. Rose and Mateo come up and it's easy to talk about how happy we are for her. I want to ask about his family's get together but worry bringing it up would be painful. Wouldn't he mention it if he wanted to talk about it?

I decide I'm too curious to hold it in.

"If I'm overstepping, absolutely tell me to shove off, but how did the celebration go? Are you okay?"

He doesn't answer right away, his attention focused on the sidewalk ahead of him. Grief replaces levity and the edges of his mouth turn downward as he rubs his forehead with his hand.

"It was difficult," he sighs, "at first. I'm not sure anybody really knew what to say or do. It's easy to be sad when thinking about the death of a loved one. It's a lot harder to be happy. Then I was thinking about what you said and I got up to tell a story."

"Will you tell me?" He studies me, a question in his eyes, but he nods.

"When I was ten, I had a particularly bad day at school. I got a D on a test, spilled milk all over my pants, and got in a fight with another kid all in the span of an hour. He started it but I was in a bad mood so I didn't back down. We threw two punches each before we got pulled apart. He was lucky I'm not much of a fighter. I, on the other hand, ended up with a black eye the size of his fist."

"Gosh."

"Both of my parents were at work so my grandfather came to pick me up. He was so calm as the teachers told him what happened. I thought for sure he'd yell at me when we left and he'd be so mad. As soon as we stepped outside, he sat me on a bench and then he did the exact opposite of what I expected. He gave me a hug. A warm and strong hug. I had spent so much of the day being angry I practically fell apart when he did that. I cried and cried and he let me. When I finished my last sob, he said something to me I'll never forget. He said, 'son, there are a lot of reasons to be angry in this world. Everybody has anger that gets the better of them some time or another. Controlling anger is one of the hardest fights we face. What I want you to remember is you are safe, and you are loved. No matter what happens, I know you're gonna be okay. You know why? Cause you got me. You've got me here to tell you that you are smart, capable, and kind. I love you, kid. No matter what.'"

He pauses there, lost in the memory.

"I'll never forget those words. How much they meant to me. When I first found out he died, that was the moment I remembered. He promised he'd be here for me and now he wouldn't be. At least physically. I know he'll always be with me in spirit and I spend every day trying to prove I'm the man he was so certain I am."

"I'm sure he was so proud of you Jamie," we both stop and I rest my hand on his upper arm.

"Don't you hate me? I'm not sure I can count on your authority on the matter."

I focus on the sidewalk ahead of me, a little ashamed.

"I don't hate you Jamie. I hate that you hurt me. Knowing you now though, I can most certainly say you are a decent and kind human being. Look how much you've helped Rose. You didn't have to do this. You didn't have to care. Yet here you are. I see the way you are with patrons at the library. I know that a person who wasn't the things your grandfather claimed you to be, wouldn't give this a second thought. The greatest thing we can do each day is wake up and try to be the best version of ourselves. Sometimes we don't succeed and that's okay. There's always tomorrow."

"We've grown up a lot these last few years haven't we?" His smile is soft and we walk again.

"Yeah, I think we have."

Since it's a warm autumn Sunday, people fill Navy Pier to the brim. Families wander about, laughing and playing. They take pictures of the children in front of the skyline. Couples sit together with heads resting on shoulders, hands being held, kisses being exchanged. So many people from so many walks of life. I know tourist traps can be annoying and overwhelming but I think that's one of the cool things about them.

I don't know about Jamie, but I definitely feel out of place. I wonder if people see us and assume we're a couple. We amble down the pier, taking everything in and not interrupting the time and place with conversation. I never minded silence with Jamie. It was easy being with him. Minus the whole talking to his ex the whole time we dated thing.

I'm tempted to ask him more about that. Ask why he did it. If he even gave it a second thought. Did he realize or care how much he would hurt me at the time? I'm not sure I'll like the answer and I definitely don't want to bring a decent day down.

When we reach the end of the pier, we sit at a table perfect for contemplating life as you gaze out over the water. The Great Lakes are named as such for a reason. It's always been crazy to me how massive they are. Miles and miles of small dancing waves. The land you know is there on the other side isn't visible. Although, people always say if you get high enough above Lake Erie you can see Canada. I've always been a little skeptical. It's peaceful. Not as scary as oceans with their unfathomable depths and terrifying creatures.

"What are you thinking about?" Jamie drags me from my reverie.

"The deep dark heart of the ocean and how frightening it is."

"Huh. How'd you get there?"

I trace my train of thought and settle on, "I was comparing the Great Lakes to the ocean. How I prefer them. What were you thinking about?"

"My grandpa," he replies solemnly. "I miss him."

"Memory keeps him alive in your heart. I'm sure wherever he is, he misses you too."

"Do you believe in heaven Mel?"

He's focusing on the lake again, probably mulling that same question over in his head.

"No," I answer truthfully. "But I believe we're all connected to the universe in ways we can never possibly understand. It makes little sense to me that there's a big omnipotent God watching over us all and making the decisions. We come from stardust and flame and when we leave this life, we go back to it. I have to hope we find our way back to the heart of the universe."

"I'm not sure what I believe," he confesses.

"I'm sure that's difficult. I know it's comforting to have faith, especially in the face of death. In lieu of faith, the second best thing is hope. Find comfort hoping you'll reunite one way or another."

"I hope you're right," he smiles at me and I can no longer deny the tingle of joy running through me. "Thank you Melody."

"We should get going. I'm excited to try Mateo's enchiladas," I stand up and start walking before he even responds.

I hear him jogging to catch up. His pace slows and his feet march in time next to mine. For a split second, I think I feel his hand brush mine. Did I totally imagine that? Even if it was real it was definitely an accident right? It has to be. I turn my head to consider him and I could swear he's got a playful grin on his lips.

Chapter 12: What Is Going On?

"I've decided to move to Oak Park to be with Mateo."

Wait, what?

My fork is hovering right in front of my lips, my mouth open and ready to take another bite of Mateo's amazing beef enchiladas when Rose makes her announcement. She glues her gaze to mine, and it is one of intense resolve.

"Rose, are you sure?" I ask and set my fork back down. "I know you two have technically known each other a long time, but you've only reunited for the first time in decades. That's so soon."

"I've made up my mind."

Jamie and Mateo are noticeably silent. Jamie keeps looking like he's about to say something but every time he moves he stops himself.

"Is this what you want Mateo?" I turn to him.

"I've been waiting for Rose to come back into my life since the moment I left. I want nothing more than to spend the rest of my life with her."

"Look, I know you two have strong feelings for each other, but this is a drastic choice. It would be smarter to take your time, making sure this is really, truly what you want. You can talk to each other on the phone every day. But moving? It's too soon."

"It's not too soon. I knew back then and I know now. The only difference is the circumstances."

I'm at a loss. Everything about this screams rash decision but at the same time, it's clear Rose has decided. I'm only her friend. And a new, much younger friend at that. Who am I to advise her for or against this choice?

"Rose, are you sure this is what you want?" Jamie asks.

"I am one hundred percent certain," Rose responds with finality.

"Okay," we both say at the same time.

Mateo reaches out to hold her hand, and she takes his with the smile of someone who is completely and undeniably in love. How can I say anything? I know nothing of true love. Rose clearly knows what she wants and has decided. I can only imagine what it would be like to be so in love and so confident of your feelings for another person to make you upend your life.

"Of course I'll go back with the two of you to get everything in order but I'll be making plans to get back here as soon as I can."

"I'll help you with whatever you need," I say to Rose, hopeful she'll recognize my shift in support. "I just want you to be happy."

That seems to be what she needed to hear because her entire demeanor softens and her smile grows wider.

"Now, I have to muster up even more courage to tell my family," she says with a chuckle.

"We can do it together after dinner if you like," Mateo offers.

"Perfect," they gaze at each other with adoring eyes and I immediately feel like an intruder on their moment.

I catch Jamie taking them in too but I don't understand his expression. I would have guessed longing, but that's not quite right. Maybe admiring? Or maybe I'm not that good at reading facial expressions and I'm completely making it up. The world may never know.

Despite the shocking news, dinner is lovely. The food is incredible as is the company. Even Jamie. Mateo and he talk a lot about living in Chicago, both reminiscing and complaining. Rose and I mostly listen with sporadic interjections.

Mateo makes us drinks, and he makes them so well I realize too late there's a deceptive amount of alcohol in them. By the end of the night, I'm keeping myself from speaking at all. My inhibitions lower more than I would like when I drink and I have a history of speaking without thinking. There's been enough of that around Jamie without alcohol being involved.

"I'll stay here tonight," Rose tells us after we finish our hot fudge sundae dessert.

"I got a room at the hotel tonight too instead of going back into the city so I can give Mel a ride," Jamie says.

Alone. In a hotel. With Jamie.

At least we're not sharing a room. Or a bed. Wouldn't it be nice to share a bed with Jamie? I remember him being so warm. I could lay my head on his chest. He could wrap his arms around me. I'd look up at him and his face would be closer than I thought and I'd tilt my head...

Shit.

I've been watching too many movies.

"Okay," is all I say.

Rose hugs us both goodnight and we're out the door. What is happening? Does alcohol make time move faster? It definitely makes it move all wiggly. Jamie's butt is nice in those pants. He seems so sturdy and strong. I just want to reach out and touch it.

"You okay Mel?" He turns around and lines form between his eyebrows.

"Okie dokie artichokie."

Jamie raises his eyebrow then seems to realize I'm more inebriated than I let on because he says, "here, let me help you," and raises his hand out to me.

I stare at it. What does he want me to do with that? Hold it? Does he want me to hit it like a horizontal high five? It's a nice hand. Long fingers. They were nice to hold. I always felt safe when I held his hand. Like if I'd fall, he'd catch me and hold me up.

"Melody?"

My eyes move from his hand to his pupils and suddenly I'm twenty and falling headfirst into those deep warm irises like a pool of warm caramel entrapping me with their sweet stickiness.

Fuck me.

"Yeah, I'm good," I go right past his hand and climb into the car by myself.

And I only tripped once.

I hear him chuckle before moving to the driver's side. He gets in, turns on the radio, and we head off. Thank goodness for the music. I'm fairly certain if it was silent I wouldn't be able to keep myself from talking to fill the void.

"So I gotta say," Jamie says, "Rose's decision surprised me."

"Me too. I knew she had intense feelings for him but had no idea she would uproot her whole life. I'm going to miss her. She may be old but she's still my friend."

"Well, like you said, you can talk to each other on the phone all the time."

"True," my head moves with the beat of the music, "this is a good song."

"Gotcha!" he shouts and I startle, "It's Florence and the Machine."

"No, it isn't!" I give the screen a closer inspection and am immediately proved wrong. "Well, okay maybe not all of their songs are terrible."

"I usually find things aren't so black and white."

"You're not as bad as I used to think," I confess.

Oh, man. Stupid gin.

"Really?"

"Yeah. When I saw you that first day at the library I literally thought about slapping you. Like they do in the movies. I was sure the universe was playing some sort of joke on me. As much as being around you is driving me crazy, I guess I'm softening up to you a little bit. Now I just want to punch you in the arm every once in a while."

"I'm driving you crazy?" His voice is full of concern. "I'm sorry."

"It's hard Jamie. You hurt me so much and every time I see you I'm reminded of back then and how it all felt and it's a lot. It doesn't help I still find you ridiculously attractive."

I slam my mouth shut so hard it actually hurts my teeth. Goddammit. Did those words really come out of my mouth? Please tell me I'm so drunk I did that all in my head.

"Oh wow," Damn. Not so lucky.

"I'm sorry. I didn't mean to say that. It's awkward and inappropriate."

"It's okay. I can't say I've ever been mad at someone finding me attractive."

"Obviously it doesn't mean anything," I stutter.

"Obviously."

Jamie pulls into a parking spot at the hotel and stops the car.

There's a few moments of quiet before he stares me dead in the eyes and says, "For the record, I still find you ridiculously attractive too."

For the second time tonight, I'm completely taken aback by a surprise declaration. I'm drunk. What's his excuse? Is it true though? Or is he saying that because I said it first and it's less awkward to agree? It definitely wouldn't be very fun for me to say I find him incredibly attractive for him to say, "eh you're alright," with a dismissive shrug. Why do I care so much that he finds me attractive? I shouldn't, right?

"Melody?" Jamie raises his eyebrows and purses his lips.

"Goodnight," I scurry out of the car and run into the hotel and don't stop until I'm safe behind the door to my room.

I pull out my phone and call the one person who will know what to say.

"Riley," a small cry escapes me. "It hurts so much."

"What does sweetie?"

I tell her what happened with sniffles mixed in and then say, "It makes me too happy to hear he still finds me attractive and suddenly I'm having feelings for him again and that's terrifying. Why can't I get rid of feelings? They're so stupid."

"Oh honey," she laughs a little. "Alcohol has a funny way of making you sappy."

"I just don't understand him. One day he's breaking my heart and then all these years later he's saying he still finds me attractive. I know I said it first but what's wrong with him?"

"You'd have to ask him that."

"Maybe I will." I wipe my nose, stand, and start swaying. "Tomorrow. Maybe I'll ask him tomorrow."

"Get some rest. Everything will be clearer in the morning once the fog passes."

"Guys are stupid Riley," I pout.

"I know they are. Best friends are better."

"They really are," I smile. "Thanks Riley. Love you."

"Love you too. Want me to come over tomorrow? Veg out? I've got lots to tell you."

"Absolutely."

"Great, see you then."

"Goodnight."

I fall into the fluffy bed without even changing into my pajamas. One last thought crosses my mind before I fall into oblivion. I really want to have sex with Jamie.

Knock, knock, knock. More like bang, bang, bang. Who the hell is at the door and why does this bed feel significantly less comfortable than it did when I woke up yesterday morning? The memory of last night flashes in my mind and I groan and throw the pillow over my face.

The knocks come again, and I drag myself out of bed. I reach my hand out to open the door and stop so my hand is hovering a little above the metal knob. What if that's Jamie? I don't even know what I look like right now. His opinion on my attractiveness could be completely reversed by seeing my hungover bed head. I rush to the mirror and brush my hair with my fingers as quickly as I can. My makeup from the day before is smudged and dull but I splash my face with a little water and mess with it so I look presentable.

Waiting on the other side of the door is Jamie with two to-go cups of coffee and a smirk before he greets me with, "thought you could use this."

I grab the mug and try to say thank you while politely shutting the door in his face but he doesn't let me get that far before he barges in the room and sits down on Rose's bed.

"Did you need something Jamie," I throw all my stuff in my bag, only leaving out my clothes for the day.

"Nah, just wanted to make sure you were good," he takes a sip from his own cup.

"Fine and dandy. Now if you'll excuse me-,"

"I'm sorry for last night," he focuses on both hands wrapped around the coffee. "I feel like I shouldn't have said the last thing I did."

"I said it first and I think we can both agree it doesn't actually mean anything so it's no big deal."

"You literally ran away," his eyes find mine.

"I had a little too much to drink and my stomach was starting to not be kind to me," I half-lie. "I didn't think you'd appreciate me puking in your nice car."

"That's it?" He gazes at me like he knows exactly how he wants me to respond.

"Of course. What else would it be Jamie?" I give him my best doe-eyed innocent expression.

"Nothing. Nothing at all. I'll be at the car and ready to leave in forty-five minutes."

He rises from the bed with a huff and walks directly out the door without another word. Now I'm confused. What did he want me to say? There's no way in hell I'll admit to him that when I saw him on that bed I seriously wanted to push him back and hop on top while kissing him with complete abandon. Absolutely not.

Why would he even want me to admit that? There's no way he would think the same thing? Could he be?

After hurrying through my shower, I meet Jamie at the car five minutes earlier than he told me to.

"Did I do something wrong?" I ask him.

"Nope," his tone is undecipherable.

He opens the trunk and I throw my bag in before we both climb in the front and make our way to Mateo's to pick up Rose.

"I'm sorry if I made things awkward Jamie."

"It's fine, Melody."

I hate that I hate he didn't call me Mel.

"You know how people get when they're drunk. They say things they shouldn't."

"I don't think that's true," he mutters under his breath.

"What's not true?"

Jamie takes a drastic right turn and pulls into the parking lot of a bank and stops the car.

"You are completely frustrating you know that?"

"What?"

"One minute you hate me, the next you're telling me how hot you think I am. What does that mean?"

"Um, I-" I sputter but don't know what to say.

"You know what?"

"What?"

I was a thousand percent sure Jamie was going to go on a rant about how annoying I am and how glad he was he broke up with me when he did because I'm insufferable.

He doesn't do that. Instead, Jamie looks like he's about to say something, then shakes his head once before leaning over, softly grabbing the sides of my head with both his hands and does the last thing I thought he'd do.

He kisses me.

I'm so startled by his actions I don't react to his lips pressing against mine at first but then my brain completely shuts off and I let my body take over. My whole body leans into his and our lips move in sync with each other. I set my hand on the back of his neck so I can pull him closer to me and kiss him deeper. A force I have no control over fuels each moment we touch but all I care about at this point is that it feels fucking amazing. Like I've been deprived of water for months and suddenly, with only a kiss, life flows through my body.

I pull away to take a breath and apparently that's enough for oxygen to return electricity to my higher functions because I don't lean forward again. I stare at him as he stares at me. Both of our breathing is heavy and his hands are hanging in the air like he doesn't know what to do with them.

"Why did you do that Jamie?" My voice is soft but strained.

"Because I really, really wanted to, and I was pretty sure you wanted me to too. I'm very sorry if I was wrong."

He stares off through the windshield.

"You weren't wrong."

He catches sight of me and if I had to guess it looks like there's hope in his eyes so I continue with, "but that doesn't mean it was a good idea."

"Why not?"

His question is loaded with surety and confidence, and it's infuriating.

"You know why Jamie! You're my ex! We've been through this before and you may recall it didn't end well. Not to mention I technically have a boyfriend which makes me officially a terrible person."

I throw my head in my hands and am tempted to cry but I hold it in.

"Technically?"

"That is so not the point of what I said Jamie," I throw my hands up in exasperation.

"Sorry," he turns back to the windshield and puts his hand on the steering wheel and drives again.

"It's messy. And complicated. What would it even mean?"

"I don't know," his voice is a whisper.

"Obviously there's no denying the attraction, but I can't do meaningless, Jamie. Especially with you."

"Mel, I don't think you understand."

"No, I do Jamie," I cut him off. "Whatever just happened was a fluke of temptation and I know it meant nothing to you and I can't do that so it can't happen again."

"But-" Jamie starts again but I stop him.

"No buts," I shake my head. "Let's pretend it didn't happen."

Jamie gives a curt nod and then focuses intently on the road. The silence is deafening but I've run out of things to say. How in the hell are we going to make it through the next five and a half hours?

Despite my firm words, I keep replaying the kiss in my head. I can never admit it out loud but it was incredible. After all this time kissing Sebastian and feeling nothing but mediocrity, it was as though the sky parted and the sun showed through to give light to that moment and make it utterly spectacular. I always thought kissing him was amazing when we were dating but this was something else.

How can something be so amazing and so horrible at the same time? I can't even process what happened because I have no idea where it came from or what it meant and there's no way I can talk to him more about it. Can I? I know I at least need time to think about it and figure out what it meant to me because I have no friggin' clue. Riley is going to lose it when I tell her.

Rose is waiting outside with her bags when we pull into Mateo's driveway. She waves to us with absolute glee. She's the purest definition of young at heart I've ever seen. I hop out of the car at the exact moment Jamie stops and grab her bags to put in the trunk.

"Why don't you sit in the front with Jamie, Rose," I shut the back door, "I'm sure it'll be much more comfortable."

"That's okay," Rose tries to reject the offer but I don't let her get the chance to actually say no because I climb in the backseat before she finishes.

"Don't let Jamie hog the music!" I shout as she opens the door to get in the passenger seat. "And you know what, I didn't have a great night of sleep so I'm going to put my headphones in and try to nap. If you need me to drive, go ahead and wake me up."

"Okay sweetie," Rose smiles at me and Jamie only nods.

Once the music blares through my ears, I finally feel like I can calm down, breathe, and absolutely pretend the kiss with Jamie didn't happen. I close my eyes and lay my head on the window but I don't sleep. Instead, I drown myself in the music and picture the songs as movies in my mind.

The five hours fly by and soon we're pulling up in front of Rose's house. During the drive, I only spoke to Jamie and Rose during our brief stop for gas and lunch. I didn't have the wherewithal to even glance at Jamie. I noticed him not-so-subtly glancing at me more than once in the rearview mirror once I opened my eyes.

"I know you're worried I'm making a rash decision but I know what I want," Rose says as I walk her inside.

"I just don't want you to get hurt," I tell her.

"I'm old Melody," she chuckles. "I want to live my life to the fullest while I've still got it. Whether I spend ten days with Mateo or ten more years, it will be worth it. Love is always worth it."

"How do you know it's love?"

Rose thinks about it for a moment before responding, "He makes me feel seen. As though he understands and appreciates every part of me, both good and bad. That no matter what comes, he'll be there for me to lean on and help me push through. It's hard to believe, but to me, love is simple. Love is someone who brings you peace, comfort, and most of all the feeling of safety."

"Thank you Rose," I hug her and set her things on the inside of the door. "Let me know what you need help with for the move. I'll do whatever I can for you."

"I appreciate it," she waves goodbye and I head back to the car.

Jamie's checking his phone when I get back in the front seat. He says nothing to me as he drives toward my apartment. I don't blame him. I wouldn't know what to say to him either. In no time at all, we're in front of my home and I'm eager to run away from him.

"Mel, let me just say," he begins once he puts the car in park, "I'm sorry for what happened earlier. Clearly it was a mistake and I never want to hurt you again."

I blink. Then I blink again. That is not what I expected him to say at all.

"It's okay Jamie," I sigh and open the door. "Maybe in another life, in different circumstances, everything would be different."

I shut the door in his face.

Chapter 13: Autumn Leaves

The following week at work flies by. I see little of Rose because she's busy getting everything in order before she moves to Illinois. Jamie and I avoid each other like the plague. Half of the time I try to pretend the kiss didn't even happen, and the other half I replay it over and over in my head. I tell myself it's because I'm trying to understand it but actually it's because it was amazing I can't stop thinking about it.

The day we got home, Riley came over in the evening and thank goodness she did because I spent the hours in between pacing and spiraling, trying to figure out what the fuck had happened.

"He did what?" Riley exclaimed when I told her.

"He kissed me. Out of nowhere. I thought he was going to tell me how much he hated me and instead he kisses me."

"They do say there's a fine line between love and hate," Riley chuckled as she handed me my bowl of ice cream and sat down.

"I don't know what to do. I thought the most difficult thing about working with Jamie was awkwardly reliving our past every day but instead we're fighting attraction? What the fuck is even happening?"

"Oh sweetie," Riley hugged me. "You guys dated for a reason. You're attracted to him right? Both then and now?"

"Yeah," I sighed. "A little too attracted."

"Then is it really that surprising he's in a similar boat?"

"I guess not," I pouted, "but he broke my heart!"

"Maybe that's all the reason to use him for some tension relief now," she teased.

"You can't be serious?"

"I am a little," she shrugged. "I know you told him you can't do meaningless sex but why not? You are in control of yourself and your feelings. Friends with benefits is a thing for a reason. Why not have a little fun?"

I actually considered it. The only thing holding me back is that I'm not convinced I could push away my feelings for him. Our relationship didn't end because I stopped liking him. It ended because he stopped wanting me. Those feelings are still there, even if they're buried deep inside and hidden behind a thin veil of heartbreak and contempt.

Somehow, Riley managed to contain her own big news that she and Jackson had done the deed.

"I can't believe you held that in while you let me go on and on about kissing Jamie!"

"He's so wonderful Mel," Riley squeezed her pillow tightly and gushed about how kind and caring he was.

"I'm so glad you found someone who makes you feel that way," I told her.

"I wish you had that. Is Sebastian not?"

"I've decided to break up with him," I hug my knees. "I decided before I kissed Jamie but it was further proof the passion isn't there and it's not enough for me."

"When are you going to do it?"

"We had plans to meet up at the Harvest Festival this weekend so I was thinking I'd do it there."

"Jackson and I are going to that. You can hang out with us after if you want."

"We'll see how it goes. Hopefully, he feels similarly and it'll be a clean break."

"You think so?" She asks.

"I don't, but here's hoping."

The Harvest Festival is here and I'm a bundle of nerves disguised as a human being. I've never actually broken up with anyone before so I keep going back and forth on what I'm going to say.

I recall Jamie's break up with me and despite how much it hurt then; it was pretty quick, easy, and to the point. Heartless, if you will. I swallow the bitterness and hope I can avoid that with Sebastian.

The Harvest Festival is being hosted at Lakeview Park. The leaves have recently hit the peak of their color now that it's mid-October and it all feels like a dream. Or a movie. Either way, everything feels cozy and warm despite the chill coming off the lake. I'm bundled up in my favorite maroon cable-knit sweater with a light brown faux suede jacket, skinny jeans, and brown ankle boots. I thought about wearing something less fun to break up with Sebastian but the whole autumn vibe was too tempting to pass up.

Sebastian is meeting me at six so Riley, Jackson, and I came earlier in the day to enjoy the festivities before I ruin the evening for both of us. I've been running scenarios through my head all day; good, bad, and awful. I've no idea what to expect and it's driving me mad.

To get out of my head I dive into all the fun activities and food. My first stop is the donut stand to try all the different varieties including apple cinnamon, pumpkin spice, salted caramel, and maple delight. Right next door is the perfect spot for the hot apple cider booth and I get the largest cup I can.

Riley and Jackson wander a few steps behind me the whole time being cute as all get out. She's got her witchy eyeglasses on today which fit the theme perfectly and match well with her black dress and purple tights. Jackson covered up his polo with a nice blue vest. They're both so cute it's hard to hold back a little jealousy.

"Hey Jamie!" I hear Jackson shout and I whip around so fast I lose my footing and fall onto a hay bale.

"Mel, are you okay?" Riley rushes to my side and helps me stand up.

Riley and I brush our hands over my back and butt and pull off all the pieces of straw we can before Jamie reaches us. Jackson gives him a bro welcome with a hand grab and quick man hug when he gets to us.

Jamie turns to me with an awkward smile. His eyes move up to my head and his smile gets bigger as he reaches over and plucks a piece of straw out of my hair.

"Awesome, thank you," the sarcasm drips from my mouth and I take the straw from his hands.

I try to avoid touching him but our fingers brush and I can't stop the goosebumps from popping up on my arms and the back of my neck.

"You know Melody. This is my girlfriend Riley," Jackson introduces her.

"Girlfriend?" Riley turns to him in surprise.

Jackson throws his hand over his mouth and gives her a stupid grin before telling her, "I was planning on asking you officially and it just came out. I'm sorry if it's too soon."

"No, I'd love to be your girlfriend," Riley gets up on her tiptoes to wrap her arms around his neck to give him a passionate kiss.

Jamie and I stand there awkwardly, both looking in opposite directions from the grand display of affection.

"Are you here alone?" Jackson asks Jamie once they pull away from each other.

"Yeah, I just came to check out the festival," he swivels his head around at all the attractions and booths, "I didn't have any definite plans."

"Why don't you join us and Mel?" Riley offers with a look of sneaky innocence.

"Oh, I don't want to intrude," Jamie waves her away politely.

"You won't be," Riley grabs Jackson's hand and starts walking away before shouting over her shoulder, "Mel needs a buddy, anyway."

"I'm sorry about that," I rub the back of my neck and cringe. "You really don't have to stick around. Please do your own thing."

"Is your boyfriend here," Jamie asks with a bite to his voice.

"He's coming later," I admit but feel the need to continue with, "I'm breaking up with him tonight."

His head whips around faster than I did earlier and then he says, "Oh yeah? Why?"

I press my lips together and tilt my head to give him a look of admonishment.

"Sorry, none of my business," he puts his hands in his pocket.

Without either of us actually agreeing to stay together, we wander through the festival, a little way behind Riley and Jackson. We end up first at the pumpkin patch, mostly filled with parents and their children but there are a lot of couples too. Riley and Jackson immediately start picking out pumpkins to carve later.

"Are you going to get one?" Jamie asks me.

"Maybe. I hate carving pumpkins though so it would just be for decoration."

"Who hates carving pumpkins?" He scans me like I grew a third head.

"It's so messy," I scrunch my nose up and make a face. "They don't last very long and when they start rotting on your front porch, it smells bad and attracts a lot of animals."

"True," he laughs while bending down. "To each their own. It's worth it so I can get the seeds and roast them."

"Those are good aren't they?" I smile at him.

"I think this one's great," he picks up and hands me the most perfectly round pumpkin. "It'll be a great decoration."

Jamie finds one for himself, and we head to the table to pay for our pumpkins. Before I get the chance to take care of my own, he gives the person money for both of us and says, "please, let me. Payment for putting up with me in Chicago."

"You don't have to do that," I try to stop him but he skirts my hand and makes sure the attendant takes the cash. "Thank you, Jamie."

Riley and Jackson make their way back to us. Jackson and Jamie offer to take our pumpkins back to the car and we wave them off, happy not to have to lug the sizable vegetables around the rest of the day.

"Why did you invite him to hang around us?" I turn on Riley.

"Why not?" She shrugs. "I think it'll be good for you. You need to decide to be friends with him in order to make work not awkward or decide to be *friends* with him and have yourself a little fun. Either way, I don't expect ignoring him is an option."

"It's been working okay for me this week," I grumble.

"If you say so," she glances at me knowingly.

I don't even have to tell her that even though we ignored each other all week, every time he was in the vicinity, my eyes would find him and linger. I've been lying to myself about it. And about the fact I've noticed his eyes lingering too.

I hate this. There's so much confusion and frustration and every time I think I know what to do, I overthink it and can't make up my mind. It's a miracle I decided to break up with Sebastian. Let's hope I don't rethink it between now and six and completely screw it up.

The boys find us again, and we get back to meandering through the festival. As we pass by the pie baking and eating contests, I wish I had known to tell Rose to enter her apple pie. She would have for sure won. We each take a sample and cast votes. My favorite is the cherry crisp while Jamie, Jackson, and Riley agree on the maple walnut with pretty pastry leaves on top.

There's so many people enjoying the festival and the energy is so festive and fun. Children run around laughing and eating caramel apples and popcorn. They play in piles of fallen leaves, throwing them up in the air to watch them fall back to the ground. A little girl with pigtails and a laugh that sounds like the twinkling wind on a warm day runs by me with hands clutching red leaves and her father chasing her. The hayride goes by full of families and couples enjoying the view of Lake Erie. I'm not sure the atmosphere could have been more perfect.

I observe Riley and Jackson and jealousy runs through my body like an invasive ivy. It takes root and settles in all my hidden crevices. I notice Jamie watching me and the jealousy turns to yearning. I wish we had never met five years ago. Never knew each other or even dated. Maybe things would be different now. All this time I've focused on him breaking my heart back then and now I'm faced with putting our past behind us in favor of something new. Why do I have to want him so much?

Jamie notices me watching him and raises his eyebrows in question. What is the question? Is he wondering what I'm thinking about? Is he thinking about the kiss and curious about whether I'm thinking about it too? Maybe he's questioning if I'm a lunatic because I'm standing here staring off into space, most likely with a weird facial expression. Ugh.

The four of us head over to the stage where a folk band is playing. I usually hate the sound of violins but there's something magical about a fiddle player and their string playing brethren. Like I could get caught up in a magic spell that will make me dance and never stop, lost in the music until I disappear from the Earth entirely.

We settle on bales of hay drinking spiked apple cider, and for a moment I feel so calm. Like there was nothing bad in the world and no matter what happens, I'm going to be okay. The feeling lasts about thirty minutes. Then I see Sebastian.

He pops up in the corner of my eye and I could have sworn when I first caught sight of him he looked angry. Viscerally angry. Then I see him again after someone walks by him, and he has a calm smile on his face and I'm sure I must be losing it. More likely the spiked cider is stronger than I thought.

I walk away from my friends and meet Sebastian by a kid's book version of a scarecrow with rosy cheeks and a thin grin.

"Hey," I try to give him my full smile but knowing what I have to do makes it hard to pull off.

"Hi. Was that your coworker you were sitting with? Jamie right?"

"Uh, yeah. We just ran into each other."

"Hm, gotcha. So what do you want to do first?"

"Actually, I was hoping we could talk?"

"Sure," he leads me away from the scarecrow and we sit on a bench facing the lake.

Do I really have to break up with him when there's such a pleasant view?

"What did you want to talk about?"

The moment's here and I'm still not sure what I'm going to say. I don't want to hurt him. He's been so nice. Riley told me to keep it sweet, simple, and to the point. Maybe I should lie and say I'm moving very far away. It would be super awkward though if he came into the library and found out I was lying.

"Mel?" He looks confused in a sweet sort of way with his head tilted and eyebrows slightly furrowed while he sets his hand on my thigh.

Here I go.

"Sebastian," I rest my hand on top of his, "you've been so amazing and sweet this whole time and I've been so lucky to have met you but I don't think this is working out."

"What?"

He pulls his hand from my thigh and his furrow deepens with his mouth set in a thin but firm line.

"I'm sorry. You're so kind and I'm so lucky to have met you but I don't think we're right for each other."

"Is there someone else?" A shadow passes over his face and for a moment I'm worried about how he's taking this.

"No, there's no one else. I've been thinking about what I want and this isn't it."

He sits for a moment, still and silent, taking my words in. He's staring at me like he's trying to read my mind or understand more from my facial features than the words coming out of my mouth.

"I understand," he stands up and turns away from me.

"You do?" It's not what I expected him to say but I'm happy to hear it. "I'm so glad. I really hope we can stay friends."

"Yeah, me too," he turns back to me and his smile is not quite right.

If I had to put words to it, I would say it reminds me of The Joker. Calculating and a little unhinged.

"Um, okay. Sorry again Sebastian, I'll see you later."

I leave him standing there and hurry back to my friends. Riley watches me as I approach and immediately comes over to me.

"You okay, sweetie?"

"I don't know. It was weird."

"He didn't take it well?" Riley pulls me to the side.

"He did," I turn back around and he's gone, "but something felt off. I don't know."

I shake my head and my eyes sweep the area to check if he's still hanging around but he seems to have disappeared.

"I think I'm just going to head home," I turn back and say it loud enough for all three to hear.

"Oh," Riley's eyes swivel from me to Jackson, clearly torn and that's when I remember we all came here together.

"Don't worry about me," I tell her, "I'll catch an Uber."

"Actually," Jamie stands, "I was going to head home soon, anyway. I can give you a ride."

"You don't have to."

"I don't mind."

"Okay, sure..." I hug Riley and thank Jackson for letting me tag along and head away from the happy couple with Jamie.

I follow him to his car and climb into the front seat like I did less than a week ago. I feel drained from breaking up with Sebastian. Even though, by anyone else's standards it went well, something didn't feel right about the whole situation. Oh well, I'm sure I'm imagining it and everything's fine. I'll feel better in the morning.

"You okay?" Jamie asks as he pulls out of the parking lot.

"I think so," I shrug. "It went fine I guess. Maybe I just feel bad."

"You shouldn't." Jamie states firmly.

"Oh? How do you know? I can tell he had strong feelings for me. The last thing I want to do is hurt him."

"You deserve the best Mel. Don't settle for less."

"What does that even mean Jamie?" I sigh in frustration. "I don't even know what the fuck I want. Sebastian was nice and kind and good to me. Everything I should want. It doesn't make sense."

My head falls on the window and I close my eyes hoping Jamie stops talking to me. I'm just done. I'm done with awkward. I'm done with confusion. I'm done with uncertainty. This crazy movie plot I'm living in has zapped my energy. I've got to leave it all behind me.

"I know you don't have any reason to listen to me Mel," he says when he pulls up in front of my complex, "and I don't blame you for that. But if there's one thing you hear, let it be this. You're so smart and kind. You want to see the good in everybody and everything and it's beautiful. You're beautiful. You deserve nothing but happiness and peace and I know someday you're going to get it."

His words hit me like a blow to my chest. Even when we were dating, he never said anything like that. My initial reaction is to think he's making it up to make me feel better but then I gaze in his eyes and I know he believes that about me without a doubt.

Tears well up behind my eyes and start spilling onto my cheeks.

"Shit Mel. I'm sorry. I didn't mean to make you upset."

"You didn't," I wipe the tears away and sniffle. "I've got to go."

I run from the car and inside my home. All my feelings are too big for me right now. I want to be so angry at him. Why does he think he has the right to say things like that? He literally broke my heart five years ago and now he's kissing me and telling me I'm beautiful? What the actual fuck? I've literally never had a guy say something like that to me though. There's no way I can actually be mad at him.

I grab Lucy when I get inside the door and pull her close to me and squeeze her. She gives a "mrow" of protest but gives into it when she realizes I'm crying and not letting go. Once the tears pass. I let her go, and she settles on my lap and kneads my stomach with loud purrs.

"What am I going to do Lucy?"

"Mrow," She purrs louder.

We both fall asleep on the couch and that night I dream of running away from a monster with a smile.

Rebekah Santoro

Chapter 14: Giving In

"You don't look so good," Jackson comments when I get to the information desk in the morning.

"Thank you for that," I say with extra grumpiness. "I slept on the couch the whole night and I had bad dreams."

"Sorry," he grimaces. "Hopefully the day goes by quickly for you."

To his credit, the morning does go by fairly fast but as soon as the clock strikes noon, it starts to feel like I'm wading through mud and sludge trying to get to the end of the day.

"Is this day ever going to end?" I throw my head on my arms on top of the desk.

"Melody," Jackson says my name with weariness.

"I just need a minute," I groan.

"Melody," that is not Jackson's voice.

I glance up and from my arms and am greeted by a huge bouquet of roses in front of familiar bright red hair.

"Sebastian, what are you doing here?" I raise myself but take a step back to keep my distance.

"Look," he moves the roses so his face becomes visible and it's the same smile as last night before I broke up with him, "I know you said this wasn't right but I know I can prove you wrong. I'm in love with you Melody!"

"I'm really sorry Sebastian," I turn to Jackson and he's sitting there stunned which is the exact opposite of helpful. "I just don't feel the same way."

"Please give me a second chance," he begs and somehow he grows bigger and gets closer to me even though there's a desk between us.

"Please go Sebastian," I plead. "I didn't want to hurt you but you're not what I want."

"I knew it," he starts shaking his head and throws the roses on the desk in front of me. "I knew there was someone else."

"There isn't," I throw my hands up and I'm starting to realize my words are falling on deaf ears. "Please Sebastian."

"She asked you to go," Jamie does his magical appearing act and I've never been so grateful to have him show up.

"I love you Melody," he whimpers pathetically and tries to walk around the desk, "please give me a second chance."

Jamie steps in front of me and crosses his arms before saying, "Leave. Now."

Jackson stands now too and plants himself next to Jamie. Sebastian seems to get the hint, and it's his turn to throw his hands up in surrender.

"I know I can change your mind Melody," he says as he backs away. "You'll see."

I watch him walk out the door and don't move a muscle until it slides all the way shut. I release the breath I didn't realize I was holding.

"Are you okay?" Jamie turns around and his expression has transformed from angry and protective to calm and worried.

"I think so," I sit back down in my chair and shake my head. "What in the hell just happened?"

"Clearly he didn't take the breakup as well as you were hoping," Jackson says sardonically.

"Clearly," Jamie scoffs.

My focus turns to the bouquet of roses laying on the desk haphazardly. The two guys see them too and Jamie picks them up.

"Want me to get rid of them?" he asks.

"Please," a shiver runs through my whole body.

Jamie disappears with the flowers and I sit back down. The idea of staying at work for even ten more minutes makes me want to scream. I stand up and walk over to Grace's office.

"Knock knock," I announce myself.

"Yes?" Grace spins around in her chair.

"I've had a sudden bout of nausea and I'm feeling pretty crappy. Is it okay if I head home for the day?"

"Oh I'm sorry to hear that," she frowns. "Of course. Go get some rest. You don't look so great."

"Thanks," I leave her office and quickly grab my stuff from the info desk.

"Heading home?" Jackson asks. "I don't blame you after that."

"Yeah. I need to throw on my pj's and get beneath a pile of blankets with cookies and snacks and not come out for a few days."

"Everything will be better tomorrow," he gets up and hugs me and I'm thankful I've found another new friend in Jackson.

He's such a good guy and I know he'll be great for Riley.

"I certainly hope so," I give him a smile but it doesn't reach my eyes.

I think about waiting for Jamie to come back so I can thank him for his help but all I want is to get out of here and go home. So I do. From the front door of the library to my car I can't shake the feeling someone is watching me. I scan the whole parking lot to make sure Sebastian isn't hanging around but I don't see him. I'm already holding the car key in between my fingers in case and I hold my breath until I'm sitting in the driver's seat with the doors locked. I speed out of the parking lot.

The rest of the night I feel completely on edge and jittery. I'm tempted to go stay at Riley's but I don't actually want to go anywhere. I texted her to let her know what happened and she offered to come over after work. I told her not to though because I know she and Jackson have plans tonight and I don't need to ruin her night with any more of my drama.

Lucy stays near my side the whole night and helps me feel better. Her and double chocolate chip cookies. I've thought a few times about getting her certified as an emotional support animal because she has a magical way of making me feel better when I'm extra anxious. Somehow she always knows when I need her to lay directly on top of my chest with her healing purrs.

At six there's a knock on my door. My heart speeds up at the thought it might be Sebastian. Then I realize it's probably Riley surprising me despite me telling her not to come over here.

"I told you to go on your date, Riley," I say as I swing the door open.

"I hope it's okay I'm here."

It's Jamie's face that greets me on the other side. He's got his arms extended and is holding out a pint of fudge brownie ice cream.

"Hi Jamie."

Does my voice sound weird and breathy?

What is he doing here?

I really want that ice cream.

"It's okay," I step to the side to let him know he can come in.

"I just wanted to check on you. You left before I got back this afternoon and I was worried."

"I'm fine," I grab a spoon from the kitchen and settle on the couch with my ice cream. "It was just a little jarring. I had no idea he would do that. Or why."

"Clearly he knew what he was losing," he smiles at me sweetly.

"Do you really think I'm beautiful Jamie?" I ask as I eat a particularly large bite of ice cream.

He seems a bit taken aback by the question at first but his face settles into resolution before he states plainly, "Absolutely I do."

I feel the blush flow through my whole body. I'm glad I decided to put on my flattering leggings and my silk red camisole. Riley's words come to the forefront of my mind. *Friends with benefits are a thing for a reason.* Jamie not only thinks I'm attractive, but he thinks I'm beautiful. I remember how our physical relationship used to be and I can no longer deny I want him. Bad.

Why *can't* I do meaningless with Jamie? Maybe our past is the exact reason why I can and should. I know how he can hurt me so I'll know to protect myself from the get-go. There's always the chance I could be completely wrong about him wanting it too, but after the week I've had, I think I might be willing to take that risk.

God, he looks good.

"Jamie," I scoot closer to him and I literally see him gulp, "do you remember that kiss from the other day?"

He nods.

"Can we try that again?"

He doesn't move for half a second. Then he nods again.

The kiss this time is slower. Instead of him initiating it, I move toward him with caution in case either of us decide to change our minds. As our lips are about to touch - I pause. One last chance for him or me to back out. He doesn't move. So I go for it.

We touch. At first it's sweet and soft. Then, the full wave of wanting hits me and I dive into him. Luckily he's strong because he catches my force and pushes back with his own. I crawl onto his lap and straddle him, forcing the kiss deeper. He responds in kind.

If I thought the kiss last week was amazing, this is on another level. Each move I make; he matches. I lace my hands through his and push my body fully up against his. We rock and moan and I know there's no stopping this. I don't want to.

He pulls away.

"Mel," his breaths are heavy and he rests his forehead on mine, "are you sure?"

"Not at all. But I know I want to, anyway."

"Thank god."

We fall back on the couch and every single stress, anxiety, and frustration melts away as our bodies come together in utter euphoria.

I wake up in the middle of the night to find I've been sleeping on the couch for the second night in a row. Instead of clutching Lucy though, Jamie has his arms wrapped around me and is sleeping peacefully. He breathes quietly and softly. In, out, in, out. I rest my head on his chest and listen as his heart is the only sound reaching me in the silence of the night.

What have I done? I feel like I should be thinking we've made a huge, terrible mistake but I don't. I'm thinking something else entirely. Damn, that was incredible.

With my eyes closed, I can pretend I've traveled through the past and it's me and him from five years ago instead of the mess that is me and him now. I place my hand on his chest, right above his heart so I can feel his heartbeat. Thump, thump, thump.

I'm sure I enjoyed this night with Jamie. I'm not sure it should happen again. Messy is a simple way of saying completely confusing and probably not a path that will lead to anything good. How could it?

What's Jamie going to think when he wakes up? I decide there's no point in fretting about it in the middle of the night. Not when I'm so comfortable. So I keep my eyes closed and let sleep take me to my dreams again and stay that way until the soft morning light is peeking through the window.

"Good morning," his soft tenor voice pulls back from dreamland and firmly into reality.

"Good morning," I echo.

Silently, we both agree to let the moment linger for a little longer. When we're ready, we sit up on the couch unsure of what to do with ourselves now. We both gather our clothes and start getting dressed.

"I'll have to leave soon so I can get ready for work," he tells me as he pulls on his pants.

"Of course," I run my hands through my hair. "Don't feel like you have to explain or stay."

"I would if I could," his tone is sincere.

"Why?" I ask with sincerity.

I thought friends with benefits didn't do the morning after? They are supposed to disappear in the quiet so as not to impede on reality. There's no breakfast. No jovial conversation about the day to come. That's couple stuff.

"I don't know I guess," he looks away as if he wanted to say something else but decided against it.

"I don't know what to say," I laugh awkwardly. "I've never really done something like this."

"Like what?" He frowns and rubs his chin.

"Friends with benefits," I sit back on the couch and pet Lucy, oblivious to him.

"Oh," Jamie's face falls.

"What? His furrowed eyebrows make it clear to me we're both confused but I don't think it's for the same reason.

"I guess I didn't think about last night that way," he picks up his shirt and throws it on.

"You didn't? How did you think about it?"

Anxiety settles deep in my stomach and it hits me like a purse full of dictionaries that Jamie and I are on completely opposite pages about what last night meant to us.

"I don't know," he shakes his head, "I guess I wasn't thinking that far ahead."

"I don't know what to say," I tell him honestly. "I thought last night was about fun and meaningless."

"I thought you couldn't do anything meaningless?" His eyebrows are furrowed and his mouth is set in a deep frown and he won't look me in the eyes.

"I-I guess I decided I could."

"I should go," he grabs his jacket and starts heading for the door.

"Jamie, wait!" I stand and follow him. "I'm so sorry if it wasn't clear what I wanted but I don't understand what else it could have been!"

He stops right before the door and turns to me and his expression has morphed. His eyebrows are no longer furrowed but his lips are still set in a frown. He stares me dead in the eye now.

"You're right," his pupils burrow into mine, "I don't know what I was thinking, and that's my fault. I guess that's what happens when you don't talk before you jump into sex. I've got to go. I'll see you at work, Mel. It's fine."

"Jamie, wait, please," I reach out to grab his arm but he shakes me away and leaves.

I stand there for a few seconds after he disappears, frozen with my arm still extended to reach out to Jamie.

What the fuck just happened?

Then there's a slow knock at the door. Tap. Tap. Tap.

I break from the spot where I'm frozen and open the door to Jamie waiting on the other side.

"I lied," he says.

"What?"

"I know exactly what I was thinking."

"You do?"

"I'm falling for you Melody."

Holy shit...What? What is happening? Apparently my silence is an invitation for him to keep going because he starts talking again.

"I've tried to deny it. Tried to push it away but I can't. Ever since you've come back into my life, I've realized you're amazing and beautiful and so unbelievably smart and kind and I can't believe I screwed it up so badly five years ago. I know you have every reason to hate me for what happened then and I can only ask you to give me another chance because I'll prove I'm not who I was back then."

"Jamie, I don't know what to say," I repeat my new catchphrase.

"You don't have to say anything right now," he grabs my hand, holds it firmly, and brings himself closer to me. "Five years ago I was such an idiot. I had been on and off with Nicole for so long, she was easy and comfortable and you were the exact opposite.

At first, I thought I could let the past go and leave Nicole behind but I was a coward. I could tell you were beginning to have strong feelings for me and it was terrifying. I didn't know how to handle it and when it became too much, I fell back into what was familiar. Nicole. I didn't want to open myself up to you. It's not that I didn't have feelings for you back then, it was that I was scared of the ones I did have and what it would mean."

My mouth is open in a small "o." I've opened and closed it a few times hoping I could think of something to say to him but I haven't gotten anything out. I can't believe what I'm hearing from Jamie. The me from five years ago would love to hear exactly what he's saying, but me now is at a complete loss. Is this real life?

"Clearly, you were thinking something completely different about last night and I totally respect that but Melody," he looks up to the sky before settling his gaze back on me, "I tried to push away these feelings again but this time I can't because I'm not afraid anymore. God, I want to be with you. I want to be there to hold you when you're sad, celebrate with you when your dreams come true, laugh, cry, and everything in between. I just want you."

"Jamie, I..." I try to think of the right words to say but how can I do that when I have no idea what I'm thinking or feeling about any of this.

"I know this was a surprise so I'm going to leave now but I need you to understand something," his body is flush against mine, "I meant every word I just said and I will spend every moment being there for you and falling even more in love with you unless you tell me you don't love me too and to leave you alone. Say those words and I'm gone but Melody...please don't."

Then he kisses me. I keep waiting for a kiss with Jamie to not be amazing but each touch is better than the last. Now that Jamie has told me how he feels, his kiss is completely uninhibited and filled with passion and I get lost in it. Even though my brain hasn't caught up with the moment, my body responds and I'm kissing him with every ounce of passion and strength I have.

When he pulls away, he gives me a meaningful stare before turning and leaving without another word.

When I shut the door a few moments later, I wander back to the couch in a daze. I grab my phone because there's only one thing I can think to do.

"What's up best friend?" Riley picks up the phone.

"So a lot has happened in not very much time," I start.

"What else could have happened?"

"Well, Jamie came over to check on me and we ended up sleeping together which was a big thing in itself and while I completely saw it as a meaningless friends with benefits thing, Jamie decided to tell me he's falling in love with me and he wants to be with me and he left a few minutes ago and I'm basically losing my mind."

"Holy shit."

"I know."

"What the fuck!"

"I know."

"What are you going to do?"

"I have no fucking clue."

Jamie gives me space at work a few hours later. I don't even see him the whole morning. After lunch, he pops up to bring me tea but doesn't linger long enough to have a conversation.

The whole day I try to figure out what I'm going to do. I know it should be as simple as do I feel the same way about him but it's not that simple. Our history makes it complicated and scary. I can't go on and pretend it didn't happen.

After work, Jamie reappears to walk me to my car and I'm boiling over with anxiety because I have no clue what to say or do.

"I have no intention of pressuring you Mel," he opens the car door. "I'll wait for you. As long as you need."

"What if you end up waiting for nothing?"

"Obviously, I'm hopeful it won't come to that, but it's your choice to make and I'll understand. Is there anything I can do to help you decide?"

"I need you to understand why it's not so easy for me to fall back into a relationship with you."

"Okay, lay it on me."

"Jamie, when you broke up with me it was terrible."

"I know," he drops his chin to his chest with hunched shoulders

"No, I don't think you do," I shut the door and lean against it so we can have a conversation without me being half in half out. "You know how when you and I started dating I had that group of friends I was always with?"

"Yeah," one of his eyebrows goes up.

"I never told you but when you and I started dating, they basically abandoned me and decided we weren't friends anymore. It sucked, but I didn't let it affect me at first because I had you. So when you broke up with me, all of a sudden I had nothing. No friends, no boyfriend, and I was states away from my family in one of the most stressful semesters of college. I was alone, scared, and emotionally vulnerable."

"Why didn't you tell me?" His face has fallen and his gaze turns back to the library.

"I was embarrassed," I shrug. "I basically spiraled into depression when we broke up and it was bad. Terrible. I didn't care about anything or anyone, especially myself. I'd cross streets without checking both ways because I decided if a car hit me, I'd finally feel something again or suddenly I wouldn't have to worry about anything anymore. I was so numb. I started going out with guys I definitely should not have and I wasn't careful. I was reckless and stupid and it's a miracle I didn't end up pregnant or with an STD. Or killed."

Rebekah Santoro

"Jesus Mel," he leans up against the car next to me but can't look me in the eye.

"I'm not telling you this to hurt you or blame you or make you feel bad," I hug myself, "I'm the only person responsible for my actions and feelings. I'm telling you so you can understand why it terrifies me to even think about having feelings for you again. I can't help but think no matter how I feel, I'll protect myself more by staying away from you."

"But you weren't worried about any of this with Sebastian?"

"The reason I was with Sebastian as long as I was is because I didn't feel remotely as much for him as I ever did for you. I knew if things ended with him I wouldn't come close to being emotionally devastated. I have to protect my heart Jamie."

He doesn't say anything for a few seconds. He watches cars pass by. What is he thinking about?

"Thank you for telling me Mel," he turns back in front of me and holds both my hands before his eyes find mine. "I do understand better now. But it doesn't change anything. I know how I feel about you and as long as you let me, I'll wait for you to feel the same way and I'll spend every day proving I won't hurt you again."

"I don't know if I will Jamie," I give him a hug because I can feel tears forming and I know if I keep looking at him they'll break free.

"I know." He pulls back and leans down to give me the softest kiss on my forehead. "Take your time. I want you to be sure of the decision you make. I'll be here."

I watch him walk away to his car and then I climb in my own and start sobbing. All of this is too much. Breaking up with Sebastian. Jamie's confession. Telling him about how horrible my mental state was back then. What the hell am I going to do? Maybe I should have stayed working at the coffee shop so none of this would have ever happened.

When I get back to the apartment, Riley is already there waiting for me with wine and brownies.

"What would I do without you?" I half laugh, half sob and hug her.

"Honestly I have no clue," she laughs and follows me inside.

"Tell me everything again. From the beginning."

So I do. I start with Jamie showing up at my door last night and end with him leaving me in the parking lot after I confessed the darkest parts of myself to him.

"Holy shit."

"I know."

I pull Lucy onto my lap against her will and chug the last of the wine in my glass.

"I don't even know what to say," she lays her head on the back of the couch and stares at the ceiling.

"Me either," I sigh. "I can't deny my feelings for him are still there. I don't think they ever left. But that's not really the question I have to answer."

"It's not?"

217

"Am I willing to risk my heart getting broken again? If it does happen, because that's always a possibility, should I be more concerned about my mental health getting as bad again because of it? I don't have the luxury of being reckless when it comes to my heart or my head."

"There is a big difference this time," Riley tells me.

"What?"

"You have me dumbass," she hits me with a pillow and Lucy jumps off my lap.

"True," I laugh. "To be completely honest, I think what I'm scared of most is just how much I feel for him. What I've felt for other guys pales in comparison to how I've always felt about Jamie. He says he's falling for me but what if he never feels as strongly for me as I do for him?"

"That's the risk you have to take when it comes to being with somebody," Riley lays her head on my shoulder.

"How do you deal with that with Jackson?"

"I take it day by day," it's her turn to pick up Lucy and make up for scaring her off the couch earlier with head scratches. "That's kind of my life philosophy. You never know what's going to happen so live each day and tackle each moment as it comes. Life is both too long and too short to worry about what tomorrow is going to bring."

"You make that sound so easy."

"Some days I do better than others," she chuckles. "No matter what happens, I'm here for you Mel. All I know is in the time I've known you; you've never felt for anyone the way you feel for Jamie. Love is always worth taking chances. Or second chances as fate may have it."

Riley's sentiment is similar to something Rose said to me when I asked her if she was sure of Mateo and all of a sudden I wish I could talk to her as well.

"Do you mind if we go on a little adventure?"

"As long as there's food involved, sure. I'm starving and as much as I love brownies, it's not exactly a hearty dinner."

Riley and I load ourselves into her car with her in the driver's seat because she only had a few sips of wine compared to my two glasses. She heads east with a quick stop at a local barbecue place to grab some food before continuing on our little adventure. The tension in my shoulders is already beginning to relieve as we get to our destination.

"I hope we're not bothering you," I say to Rose when she opens the door.

"Not at all! Come in!"

We follow Rose inside and she gestures for us to take a seat in her living room full of boxes.

"I'm sorry it's such a mess. You must be Riley. Melody has told me so much about you. It's such a pleasure to meet you."

"You too," Riley smiles at her.

"So what brought you to see me tonight?"

"I have a dilemma and I was thinking I could use your advice, Rose."

I tell her my story and she sits there taking it all in. She nods in understanding in some parts and grimaces in worry at others. By the end, she is completely still and her mouth has fallen open.

"Goodness," she says, "I think I need some tea to help all that sink in."

"I know it's a lot. Saying it all out loud makes it sound even more dramatic than I realized. I really don't know what to do."

"What's your opinion on what she should do Riley? You know Melody best."

"To be honest, I'm not exactly sure either. The romantic in me thinks she should risk it all because I know how she feels about Jamie and she deserves a great and beautiful love but as her best friend, I worry about her and don't want her to get hurt."

"Both very understandable trains of thought," she nods. "I guess my question for you Melody, is how you feel about Jamie, stronger than your fear of getting hurt by him?"

"One minute I think yes, absolutely it is, but then I remember how much he hurt me and I can't help but be scared of it happening again. Can I really trust he's changed?"

"The Jamie I've gotten to know is sweet, kind, and reliable. If it were me, I wouldn't for a second think he was capable of such a thing but I don't have the history with him to trust that sentiment."

"I saw him at the Harvest Festival Mel," Riley interjects. "The way he looked at you, that is a man completely in love. He's not twenty anymore. It's totally believable he's not the same guy he used to be. You'll have to find a way to trust your gut."

"I know," I nod. "The problem is I trust myself even less than I trust Jamie."

We spend the rest of the night helping Rose pack her things and talking about anything but Jamie.

"I can't believe you're leaving so soon," I say to Rose before we head home.

"I can hardly believe it myself," she laughs. "It's all moving so quickly. Much quicker than I expected it would. I have to have faith it's a sign I'm doing what I'm supposed to."

"I've been meaning to ask how your family reacted."

"They were worried at first too, but when I explained it all to them, they knew there was no convincing me to not do it and ultimately want me to be happy. The twins are excited to visit me in Chicago."

"Just promise me the first thing you'll do is go get a library card," I tease.

"It'll be the first thing I do," she promises.

We wave goodbye after making plans for me to come help her finish packing and to say goodbye this weekend.

"What am I going to do Riley?"

I watch the night sky as we cruise down the road parallel to Lake Erie. The stars burn so bright and beautiful. I wonder which ones have already exploded and lost their light but we're too far away to see it yet.

"Don't overthink it Mel. Follow your heart."

"I think my heart is not to be trusted."

"I think you have the best heart and it deserves to be loved."

"Thank you for being here for me Riley," I squeeze her hand.

"That's what best friends are for," she squeezes back.

At least there's one person I can be sure about right now.

Chapter 15: No Means No

My gaze finds Jamie first thing tomorrow morning. As I look him over, I try to make up my mind once and for all. Shouldn't this be easy? I either have feelings for him or I don't. That should be all that matters, right? But it isn't, and I fooled myself into believing he cared for me before. You can never fully trust anyone not to break your heart. When can you tell it's worth giving them a second chance?

I try to think of it objectively. Let's say someone is trusted to carry a precious family heirloom vase from one side of the house to the other. And they drop it. It shatters to a million pieces and it can never be put back together. Do you trust them to carry another family vase or do you say, no thank you, I'll keep it safe and protect it myself? Yet, when I personally break something, I become extra careful the next time I have to repeat the action. Does that mean

Jamie will be extra careful with my heart this time? Can I trust every other person in the world to be as careful the second time?

"Don't do it. Everyone is selfish at their core so he's bound to hurt you again," the little devil on my shoulder says.

"People change and grow. Some people are worth a second chance," the angel counters.

"You two are very unhelpful," I mutter to myself.

"What's that?" Jackson's squinting at me like I've grown a third head, and that's the moment I decide I need to banish my angel and demon forever and decide like a grown adult.

"Hey Mel," Jamie walks up to the other side of the information desk with his signature grin and leans forward to say, "I just need to-"

"Look Jamie, I'm sorry but I need more time."

"Uh, I know," he chuckles, "I need to run an update on the computers at the desk."

"Oh," I laugh awkwardly, "gotcha. Sorry. I'll get out of the way."

"What was that about?" Jackson asks as we walk away.

"Oh you know, we slept together and then he confessed he has feelings for me and is waiting for me to decide if I have feelings for him and want us to be together," I shrug. "No biggie."

"Wait, what?" Jackson says as he crosses his hands in front of his chest in a show of being taken aback.

"I shouldn't have said that at work should I? That's unprofessional."

"Don't be sorry, Riley told me something was going on but not the details. She said she couldn't divulge 'best friend secrets.'"

"You can let her know I appreciate that but you're officially my work husband so why not tell you everything?"

"It sounds like Jamie's closer to being your work husband...and actual husband."

"Oh my goodness," I put my head in my hands. "What would you do?"

"Speaking as a guy, you'd either have to be really stupid or really brave to fall for a girl you've already dated and hurt before. From what I know of Jamie, I'd venture the latter. There are no guarantees but if I had to guess, he means what he says and he'll be extra careful he won't hurt you again."

"You think?"

"I do. But what do I know? I'm still a little baffled someone as incredible as Riley likes me at all so..."

"She is pretty awesome. That reminds me, there's a duty I've been neglecting."

"What's that?"

"If you hurt my best friend, I'll kick your ass. I know I don't seem super intimidating but I'm pretty sure I could take you."

"I think you could," he laughs. "Believe me, I have no intention of hurting Riley."

"I'm sure that's what Jamie used to say too. Intention doesn't matter. Actions do."

"So what do Jamie's actions now tell you?"

Now that's a good question. What do Jamie's actions tell me? That he's been sweet and thoughtful since he's been back in my life. That he'd go out of his way to help me and be there for me and for others he cares about. Any terrible moments we've had since we've been back in each other's life have stemmed from rehashing our past. In recent memory, I can't think of him being anything but kind and considerate, even in the face of me being harsh with him.

Maybe that's all I need to know.

But I don't want to make any decision without spending at least a couple more days thinking about it. This is a big deal and I can't make it rashly.

Soon, the week is over. Jamie has given me the space I requested and by Friday morning I'm craving his presence back in my life. The memory of our recent night together lives rent free in my mind and I can't deny I want it to happen again.

Every day this week, I work on a project weeding the collection of old and uncirculated fiction books. I'm so close to being finished on Friday I decide to stay a little late to finish it up. It only takes me an extra hour but I'm happy to finish the project while it's still fresh in my mind.

When I'm done, I make sure everything's turned off and locked up. It's odd and a little creepy to be in the library by myself in the dark. It's a big enough building that each small noise makes me do a double take and I keep having the feeling someone is watching me. I'm grateful when I get to close the front door and leave it locked behind me.

I turn to the parking lot and something feels off. It's dark, so it's hard to tell if anything is amiss. Then it hits me. My car isn't the only one in the parking lot.

"Melody, please talk to me," Sebastian climbs out of the driver's seat.

"Sebastian," I keep my distance and hold on tightly to my bag, wishing I had grabbed my keys. "I have nothing else to say. I'm really sorry it didn't work out between us but it is over."

"You've got to give me another chance," he's shaking his head, "I know I can fix it. I know we're meant to be together. I love you Melody."

I can't believe this is happening. I had no way of knowing Sebastian could become so unhinged. Or delusional about our relationship. I knew he liked me more than I liked him but I had no idea he would take it this way. Or be this upset about me ending things.

"You can't know that," I implore. "You can't be in love with me, we only dated for a little while and I don't feel the same way for you."

"Please," he takes a step closer to me and I take a step back.

As soon as my foot touches the ground his expression changes. Pure rage replaces the pleading heartbroken face. I have to change tactics. There's clearly something wrong here and I can't provoke him. Will I be able to get my phone out and dial 911 without him noticing?

"You know what Sebastian, you're right."

"I am?" The anger softens enough that I hope this will work.

"Yeah," I do my best to smile, "Maybe I just didn't give it enough time."

"You're lying," the softness has retreated from his face and we're back to fury.

"I'm not! Please Sebastian, I'm sorry. Clearly, I made a mistake. I didn't realize you felt so strongly for me. That changes everything."

"You didn't realize?"

That was the wrong thing to say because he storms over to me and gets in my face.

"How could you not realize! How could you not feel how I felt about you every time we kissed! When we fucked!"

"Sebastian, I'm truly sorry. Please calm down so we can talk about this."

"Don't. Tell me. To calm down."

My whole body is shaking. I've been scared before but for the first time in my life, I'm completely overtaken by fear. Every single muscle is tense and I need to figure out where I can run. Could I make it back to the library before him? If it weren't locked, I think I could, but there wouldn't be enough time for me to unlock it and me running would probably do nothing except provoke him further so I have to make sure I can keep going. Same goes for my car. What's nearby? I can't think straight. I have no idea where anything is. I'll just have to start running.

But what if he gets in his car to follow me once I run? There's no way I can get anywhere. I'm not fast enough. I can't get away.

"Please Sebastian, forgive me. I made a huge mistake and I realize that now. I'll give you another chance if you give me one."

"You're lying," he shakes his head again.

Oh good, I'm so glad he's delusional enough to think he's in love with me and that we're meant to be together but not so crazy he can tell I'm lying. I make a mental note to work on my poker face if I survive this.

"There's somebody else isn't there?"

"No, of course not!"

Fingers crossed my face got better at lying between the last thing I said and now. Technically, it's not an actual lie as I didn't break up with Sebastian for Jamie. There you go Mel. It's not a lie. Make him believe it's not a lie.

"I don't believe you. There's got to be a reason you aren't as in love with me as I am with you."

Awesome.

"I promise Sebastian. I did not break up with you for someone else."

His body is rigid, but he tilts his head and pauses and I hope he's considering I might be telling the truth. I can't tell if he's close enough to believing it or not.

He grabs my arm.

I'll take that as a no.

"It doesn't matter. I love you Melody. You are mine and I am yours. I'll just keep you with me until you believe it too."

"Sebastian, stop. Please let me go."

He drags me toward his car. I try reaching into my purse for my phone but he notices and knocks it out of my hand. Jerking my arm as hard as I can, I try to free it from him but he's too strong and I can't break loose. I hit him with my bag and then I drop it and use my fist but it doesn't phase him enough to let go. He gets me close to his car and wraps both arms around me so I can't move.

The headlights of a car turn into the parking lot and we both turn our heads to see what's happening. The arrival of the car distracts Sebastian, and he loosens his grip enough for me to elbow him in the stomach and I attempt to get away. He grabs my arm again and pulls me back. Fuck, that hurt.

Another mental note for if I survive this; Work on my running until I can sprint like a champion.

"Sebastian, you need to let her go," Jamie's voice makes my head whip around.

"This is none of your business. Turn around and go home."

"Melody clearly wants you to let her go and you aren't. That makes it my business. Do the right thing and leave her be."

"Get the fuck away from us," Sebastian takes a step forward and makes himself stand taller.

He then pulls me tighter and closer to him. Jamie throws his hands up in surrender and takes the step back.

"Sebastian, you're making a big mistake. Do you really think this is the way to get Melody to want to be with you?"

"It doesn't matter. I'm doing what I have to do," he goes to open the door and tries to put me in the back seat but I'm able to put my hands up to stop him from shoving me in the car.

Next thing I know, I feel the entire weight of Sebastian disappear from the back of me. I flip around and gasp as two bodies fling themselves at each other. They're wrestling on the ground, each one trying to get a leg up on the other. They fall apart and each stand with both their arms ready to swing.

"Please stop this," I beg while sobbing. "Sebastian, leave him alone!"

"Is this who you left me for!" He screams. "I knew you were a lying bitch. Don't worry though. I'll make you forget him and we'll be perfect together."

"You couldn't be perfect for her no matter what you do," Jamie shouts back.

"Just stop! I don't want anyone to get hurt."

"It's a bit late for that, sweetheart!"

Sebastian sounds completely unhinged and I'm terrified for Jamie and I's safety. Sebastian swings but Jamie dodges the blow thank god. He throws another punch and this time Jamie isn't fast enough. I hear the blow land.

A loud gasp comes from my mouth, and I throw my hand over my lips. I run to him but Sebastian turns around fast and I realize he's going to come for me again. I stop and thank the universe when Jamie gets back up. He's a little wobbly though and I worry he won't be able to stay up if he takes another punch.

"Sebastian!" Jamie yells to get his attention off me.

No. Jamie. You can't get hurt. I can't lose you again.

All sense of logic leaves me and I pound my fists on Sebastian's back.

"Get. Away. From. Him!"

Sebastian swings around and his fist hits me in the cheek before I realize what's happening.

"Melody!" Jamie shouts to me as I fall to the ground.

Sebastian's large body looms over me as I lay there and fear has permeated every atom of my body. I know I don't believe in God, but whatever is out there, I'm praying to please let me and Jamie get out of this. *Please.*

"Hey asshole," Jamie says to Sebastian to grab his attention and then throws a punch with all of his bodyweight and lands it squarely on Sebastian's jaw.

He pauses in surprise and covers his chin with his hand. For a moment, I hope the blow caused him to stop and maybe he'll leave us alone. I'm not that lucky. He squares up with Jamie and starts swinging wildly. Jamie blocks the first couple but then the hits land and soon he's on the ground with Sebastian on top of him.

I get up as quick as I can and throw myself on Sebastian's back and start pounding again.

"STOP!"

Hit. Hit. Hit.

"Please stop," I sob.

Headlights fly into the parking lot accompanied by sirens and blue and red lights.

"Stop and put your hands up!" Voices shout.

The lights are enough to pull Sebastian from his vicious assault on Jamie and he throws me from his back. I land on the ground and the cement hitting my back knocks the breath from my lungs.

My head is spinning but I roll on to my stomach and start crawling.

"Jamie!" I shout.

He's not moving when I get to him. He's got blood all over his face and his eyes are closed. One of my hands lands on his chest and one cups his cheek. I can feel his heart beating and I release a breath. He only got knocked out. I shake him and his eyes flutter open.

"Jamie, are you okay? Please tell me you're okay."

"Mel...Do you think you're still going to find me attractive with my face pounded in like this?" He laughs and it turns into a cough.

"Oh my god," I lay my head on his chest and start crying.

"Hey, it's okay," his hand falls on my head. "I'm okay. You're okay."

"What were you thinking!" I lightly hit him on the chest. "What were you even doing here!"

He coughs again as he tries to sit up. He gazes past my shoulder and I turn to find a police officer loading Sebastian in the back of his car. He then walks over to us.

"Are you two okay?" He leans down to us. "I'm Officer Johnson. Can you two tell me what happened here tonight?"

I tell the officer our side of the story. He says nothing as he writes things down in his little notebook.

"Mr. Kelly told us he was defending you against this man's unwanted attention," Officer Johnson informs us.

"It was the exact opposite," I shake my head. "You have to get him away from us."

"Don't worry, we can tell he's lying, and it was obvious he was the aggressor when we showed up. We'll get the video from the library's cameras tomorrow but for now we'll take him to the station and you won't have to worry about him anytime soon. Ah, here's the ambulance. They're going to want to take you to Mercy Hospital, Mr. Washington."

"Oh, I don't think that's necessary," Jamie groans out.

"That's between you and them," Office Johnson stands to leave then tells us, "if there's any follow-up questions I'll be in touch. Thank you."

The paramedics rush over to us as soon as the ambulance stops. They check Jamie out first since he's the one clearly worse off. They suggest he come to the hospital to get looked over by a doctor but he says no.

"Jamie, you need to go get checked out," I insist.

"I have no interest in spending over a thousand dollars to ride in the wee-woo wagon and then spend even more at the ER to be told I've got a few cuts and maybe a concussion."

"Fine, but at least let me take you to an urgent care," I push.

He looks like he wants to say no to me too but he glances at my face and I think I must be pulling off sad and worried well enough because he relents. I help him over to my car and into the passenger seat.

We're in and out of the urgent care pretty quick. Jamie was exactly right about what the doctors were going to say.

"I've had one or two concussions," he shrugs the doctor away.

"Then you know you'll need someone to stay with you tonight and wake you up every couple of hours," the doctor says to me.

"I'll stay with him," I reply before Jamie can say he'll be fine on his own.

"As much as I love your company, you really don't have to do that Mel," he stares down at his shoes.

"Yes I do," I say firmly and then continue with, "I want to," in a softer voice.

"Okay," he grabs my hand and stares deeply into my eyes, "thank you."

Jamie gives me his address and I follow the directions on my phone to his apartment in Avon Lake. It's a small one bedroom, but it's well furnished and clean. The appliances and built-in features are nice. My apartment isn't terrible, but it's old. Ancient compared to Jamie's which seems brand spankin' new.

Jamie's only been here a few months, so the apartment is pretty sparse but there is clear evidence of Jamie's personality scattered throughout. Photos of his family and Chicago are in picture frames on the wall. He has a brand new PS5 under a massive TV with a couch right in front of it. A perfect setup for a bachelor.

"Nice place. What were you doing before you came to the library?"

"You know...corporate IT in Chicago. I started at a pretty big company right after graduation. It paid the bills."

I'm guessing the bills and then some when I think about this apartment and the brand new car.

"Why would you leave such a cushy job?"

"It wasn't what I wanted. It was soulless. Not that IT really has a soul but if I'm going to be messing with technology for someone, I'd rather do it someplace that matters."

I make sure Jamie makes it to the bedroom okay and leave him to get a shower and changed. I wander back to the living room. The wall of pictures piques my curiosity. Jamie as a kid pops out at me from a few of the photos and it makes my heart sing to know his smile hasn't changed.

I end up cursing my curiosity when I discover a group photo of him and his friends from high school. It shouldn't surprise me to see him with his arm around Nicole. As much as I've done to forget about her, she appears exactly the same as when I knew her. Well knew of her. I guess the one good thing about the whole situation was Jamie never tried to get us to hang out together and be friends.

I forgot how beautiful she is. In the picture she is petite with straight black hair and a sharp elfin-like face. Every time I saw her, I wondered what Jamie saw in me because we looked nothing alike. I was more tall oaf than petite elf. It hurt so much more when he went back to her because my first thought was 'of course he did. Why would he stay with me when he could have someone who looks like her?'

I force myself to walk away from the photo. The decision I have to make is hard enough as it is. All of those same questions I had then come flooding back and make me unbelievably insecure. What if I'm not good enough? What if he finds someone better later? What if? What if? What if? It's a wonder anybody decides anything at all.

"Do you want some tea?" Jamie walks up behind me.

"I'm pretty sure I'm the one that should make you some tea."

"Do you know where the teapot and tea are?" he raises his eyebrow.

"No, but you can tell me," I head to the kitchen and he directs me to a cabinet next to the stove. "Sit down, Jamie."

"I'm fine Mel," he obeys me anyway, "it looks worse than it is."

"The shower helped get rid of most of the blood. Seriously though, are you okay?"

"I promise I'm okay."

"I don't know what would have happened if you hadn't shown up. What were you even doing there?"

"I left my credit card in my locker," he shakes his head. "I didn't need it that bad but I decided I should go get it just in case. I was driving slowly and managed to call the cops right before he could see me as I pulled in."

"I'm glad you were there," I put water in the kettle and set it on the stove.

"The better question is, are you okay Mel? That was crazy."

"Yeah... I don't think it's hit me yet. I just wanted to get away and then he hurt you and I was worried about you. It will probably settle in a little while. I'm okay for right now."

"I can't say I blame the guy for being upset about losing you but I did not see that coming," Jamie sits on his couch.

"I didn't either but now that I actually have a chance to process it, there were things here and there that were definitely red flags. It's part of why I ended it. I didn't think it would be that bad though. He was really going to hurt me wasn't he?"

"Yeah, I think he was," Jamie's voice is solemn.

The piercing cry of the steam shooting out of the teapot interrupts the silence that follows. I run to the kitchen and pull it off the burner. I pour the boiling water over the chamomile tea bags in two separate blue mugs.

"Here," I hand one mug to him, "hopefully it'll help you relax."

"I can't stop thinking about what you told me," he admits and sips the tea, "I can't believe what a dick I was."

"I couldn't believe it either," I tease and nudge him with my shoulder. "In all seriousness though, as much as I can say you screwed up, I had my own issues too that had nothing to do with you."

"Yeah, but if I hadn't been such a selfish idiot, maybe things would have been different."

"Maybe. There's no point in what if's. We could have stayed together and I still could have become depressed for other reasons. Or you could have had sex with Nicole and that would have hurt me in a whole other way. Or maybe we could have lived happily ever after. Who knows?"

"I'm sorry Mel," he's staring into his cup, "I know I've said it before but I need to be sure you know I mean it."

"I know you do Jamie," I feel the need to lay my head on his shoulder. "It's so funny. I can't tell you the amount of times I thought about running into you again. I can remember at least three times I could have sworn I saw you in a grocery store or walking along the sidewalk and I didn't, really. For so long I was certain if it had only been a different time or place, you could have been the one for me. After a while I finally convinced myself I'd never see you again and it would only ever be a painful memory."

"Then I came back."

"Then you came back."

"I didn't plan to see you again. For all I knew you were still in Chicago. When my grandpa died, I knew I needed to be somewhere new and different and for some reason I thought of the stories you told me about growing up on Lake Erie and started googling IT jobs in the area."

"If this were a movie, and I was more of a romantic I might say the fates are spinning their tangled web," I chuckle.

"Remind me to send a thank you letter to the fates," I snap my head up when he says that and our eyes lock together.

"I've been thinking about everything I promise," I'm tempted to bring my lips to his but I hold myself back, "Give me a little more time. It feels wrong to make any choice in the wake of what happened tonight."

"Mel, listen to me. Take as long as you need. Waiting is the least I can do. Can I say one more thing?"

"Sure," I'm breathless being so close to him.

"Forgive the dramatics but since you've been back in my life, my entire world has changed so much for the better. I had fallen into what's comfortable and safe and I thought all I needed was a change in scenery. Then I saw you again and my safety bubble shattered. I was terrified at first but then your warmth and your light brought me back to life. I can't change the past but I can damn well make any future we choose to have be incredible."

I bask in his words for a few moments, not knowing how to respond to such a sentiment. I want to fall into his arms and never leave. I also want to jump his bones but I have barely enough self-control to avoid doing that at this exact moment. God, I just want him.

I have no words so I let my body do the talking. I lay a gentle kiss on his lips and linger for a few seconds. In the time that passes between the blinks of an eye, I see it all. I see him. I see me. I see us. I imagine a future that lasts forever and each minute we have together is special and full of love and passion and wonder.

Then I imagine I make the other choice. The safer choice. I say no. I protect my heart and step away from the unknown. Because all that came a second before was only a possibility. There's no certainty, and that's too terrifying to risk another broken heart. I meet somebody else to live out my happily ever after with and Jamie is never anything more than a "used to be" and "what if."

Both options are scary. Both options are a potential way forward.

What do I choose?

Reluctantly, I force the kiss to part. I know neither of us want it to end but Jamie literally got beat up a few hours ago, and a delusional ex-boyfriend attacked me so we both need rest. I take him to his bed and set alarms to go off every two hours per the doctor's orders.

"Stay with me."

"Jamie, I'm not sure that's a good idea."

"No sex. Just sleep. Stay with me."

I don't say no.

I lay in his arms and rest my head on his chest and listen to his heartbeat.

Da-dum, da-dum, da-dum.

Jamie. Jamie. Jamie.

What do I choose?

Chapter 16: A Girl and a Boy

The morning comes and I thank the universe Jamie is alright. My head never moved from his chest outside of stirring him from his slumber to confirm he doesn't have a concussion. The comforting *thump, thump, thump,* lolling me to sleep each time I had to wake him up. The eager chirps of birds pull me from sleep one last time but I don't move yet.

In the dawn of this new day, I realize so much has changed. Without me fully realizing it, so many aspects of my life differ from what I imagined they'd be only a few weeks ago. Jamie's a continuous question of *what if* and *maybe* but the time to make a decision looms. I can't leave Jamie hanging forever, despite what he says about how long he's willing to wait for me. Sebastian was definitely not what I wanted. That's more clear than ever. Is Jamie?

Let's think about what I know. The chemistry I have with Jamie is not only still there, but stronger than ever. There's the risk of getting my heart broken again but that's a risk any time you fall in love and start a new relationship. Do I think Jamie's changed? Yes.

Have I changed? I'm not so sure. Am I strong enough to put myself back together again if it doesn't work out? I think so.

The one thing I know with absolute certainty is Jamie makes me feel things like no one else does. My whole body comes alive when he's near and every touch, every word, is a jolt of electricity that explodes inside me with passion and light. He aggravates me half of the time but the other half he makes me laugh and he challenges me to be the best version of myself I can be. He's kind and caring and goes out of his way to help so many people. As long as he doesn't repeat past mistakes, how could I say no?

"Good morning," Jamie whispers as his body stirs beneath me.

"How are you feeling?" I turn my head so I can study his face.

"Like I've been beat up," he chuckles. "I've been better. I think I might have to take a day or two off work."

"Good. You should rest."

"Sounds like a plan to me," he lays his head back down and starts fake snoring.

"Hey," I put his hand in mine and interlace our fingers, "I thought maybe in a couple days when you're feeling better we could go to dinner."

The fake snoring stops.

"Dinner?"

"Yeah, I think we have some things to talk about," I lay my head back down and feel a smile light up my face.

"Yes, absolutely," He moves to sit up and groans at the effort.

"Like I said," I laugh, "in a couple days when you're feeling better."

"Okay," he lays back down.

"I should get going," I pull myself up. "I promised I'd meet Riley and Jackson for breakfast."

"You could stay with me all day. We can both pretend the rest of the world doesn't exist."

His proposition is tempting. I imagine us lying in bed all day, talking, cuddling, kissing... maybe a little more. Oh, it sounds like a dream. I'm not ready for that yet though. I think I've made my decision but I want a little extra time to digest everything that's happened so I can feel confident in my decision. Talk it over with Riley one more time to make sure I'm not doing something crazy. Plus, after what happened last night, it feels a little...quick.

"Next time," I tell him in a way I hope he understands how much I mean it. "Seriously, get some rest. Order some food, sleep a lot, heal up. There's time enough for everything else. I promise."

"I hope so," he squeezes my hand and I'm filled with excitement for what's coming.

I stand and lean to give him a soft peck that lingers for a half second and I savor it. I don't want to break the connection but I know it's what is right for now.

"I'll see you soon," he whispers to me with a sweet smile.

"If you need anything, let me know."

"The only thing I need is you," his tone has shifted to complete seriousness and the only thing I know how to do is give an awkward laugh in response.

"And my car," his mouth pinches as he realizes this.

"Right," I scrunch my mouth up in thought before replying, "I can have Riley drive me to the library and we can drop it off to you later if you want."

"You don't have to," he waves me away, "I'm sure I'll be well enough to go grab it."

"I don't mind. It's the least I can do after last night."

"Thank you, Mel."

"I'll see you soon," I repeat back to him and make my way out of his apartment after he tells me where to find his car key.

"What the fuck?" Riley practically shouts when I tell her about the events of the night before.

Jackson is sitting there slack jawed and I haven't even gotten to the worst of it. When I do, Riley is sitting there with smoke practically coming out her nostrils. Jackson's look has stayed much the same but his eyebrows inched bit by bit upwards as the story progressed until I'm pretty sure they became a part of his hairline.

"I can't believe you didn't call me last night," Riley shakes her head as she dives into her ham, cheese, and spinach omelet.

"It all went so fast," I shrug. "I can't believe it happened at all."

"I mean Sebastian had been weird when he came into the library," Jackson comments, "but I would have never thought..."

"Me either," I eat my raspberry pancakes with lemon drizzle. "I'm just lucky Jamie showed up when he did. Who knows what would have happened if he hadn't."

"Your knight in shining armor," Riley winks. "How heroic!"

"He was amazing. I've never been so scared in my life."

"I can only imagine," Jackson comments. "I'm not sure if I'd be brave enough to do what he did."

"I think you would," Riley blushes and reaches for his hand. "Don't sell yourself short."

We all focus on eating our breakfast after that. I don't want to think about Sebastian ever again. I was ready to leave him behind when I broke up with him but after last night I don't want him to have any space in my brain at all.

"I've decided," I tell them casually.

Riley stops moving with her fork hanging in front of her mouth before asking, "About Jamie?"

"Yeah," I nod and keep eating, "I think I'm going to give us a chance."

"Oh, my goodness!" Riley squeals. "This is so exciting. You needed to make this decision on your own but I'm so glad. I think it's the right one."

"Not that it matters what I think but I think you are too," Jackson says.

"It's crazy," I say and put my fork down. "I never would have imagined this would happen. That I'd even see him again. Me from five years ago would be absolutely losing it."

"I'm sure Jamie from five years ago would be too."

"By the way, he left his car at the library because I drove him to urgent care. I know you guys are doing things today but can you run me over there tomorrow morning Riley?"

"Of course. I want to hug him in person for saving my best friend, anyway."

I leave Riley and Jackson to their day of fun. They're going to the Cleveland Museum of Art and then to a nice early dinner in the city. I imagine going on a cute date like that with Jamie and almost audibly squeal in excitement. I text Jamie to let him know he'd get his car back in the morning before going home to spend the day in my pajamas and snuggling with Lucy.

"It was such an amazing day Mel," Riley gushes when she picks me up the next morning. "I couldn't have asked for anything more perfect. I like him so much."

"I'm so glad you found each other. We'll have to go on some double dates. I don't want to get my hopes up too much but I foresee some cute Christmas markets in our future."

"That would be amazing! Then we'll get married and have babies at the same time and all be best friends!"

"Okay, now I think we're really getting ahead of ourselves," I burst out in laughter.

As we pull into the parking lot of the library, flashbacks from the other night burst through my mind. I've never seen anyone with such rage before, let alone had that anger targeted at me. Was there something I could have done differently? Some way I could have foreseen this happening so I could avoid it? I didn't want to hurt Sebastian, but judging from his reaction, there was no way any relationship with him could continue or end well.

I hurry from Riley's car into Jamie's and rush out of the lot with my best friend following me. God, I hope I don't feel like this every time I go to work now. Will I always be afraid Sebastian could be lurking around every corner? That one day he'll come back to the library even angrier than before? I have no idea what's going to happen to him but I'm realizing it may always be a possibility he'll show back up in my life and that's scary.

Am I going to need to testify against him in court? Probably. God, what is that going to be like? Will I be able to stand up in front of a judge and jury and relive that night? Even if he goes to jail, it probably won't be forever. He could count down the days until he's out and then come after me again. Will I have to move to get away from him?

My thoughts are running in circles about this by the time we get to Jamie's complex. Riley and I park side by side and make our way toward Jamie's door. I almost forgot how close to Halloween it is. Ghosts, bats, cobwebs, pumpkins, and other spooky decorations adorn many of the doors.

"This place is nice," Riley comments halfway through the parking lot.

"Right?"

Jamie's place is on the ground floor and in the light of day I realize the sliding glass doors in his living room lead to a small patio. The doors are open since it's unseasonably warm for late October. The curtains are also pulled back and I sneak a peek inside and realize there are two bodies standing near the doors.

"Who's that?" Riley asks.

My heart sinks to the bottom of my stomach. I feel as though the ground beneath my feet has disappeared and I'm falling into a dark abyss. That face. When I saw Jamie for the first time at the library, memories of hurt bombarded me. It's nothing compared to seeing Jamie now with her.

"That would be Nicole," I tell Riley. "Jamie's ex who he cheated on me with and left me for."

"You have got to be completely shitting me," Riley grabs my hand.

"I wish I could joke about that."

They appear to just be talking at first. Fuck she looks amazing. How does she still look like that? He leans over and hugs her. Riley gasps so I don't have to.

"What the fuck," she says.

"I should've known," I shake my head. "How could I be so stupid? Again."

"Wait a minute Mel," Riley pulls me to the side so we're not in plain view of the window.

Not that it matters. Their attention is clearly glued to each other.

"I'm sure it's not how it looks. Jamie's changed, remember."

"Yeah, that's what I kept telling myself five years ago. It doesn't even matter. This is proof he hasn't changed. That no matter what, those two just can't keep away from each other. I would be an idiot to let him back into my life knowing that."

"Mel, wait," I throw the keys under the doormat, and storm back to Riley's car, "you should talk to him before you jump to conclusions."

"No," I get in the passenger seat and slam the door. "There's no point. Even if nothing happens between them right now, it was fate for me to see it. The universe is reminding me Jamie and I aren't meant to be. Him and Nicole are. They always find their way back to each other. They have since high school. Who am I to argue with the universe?"

"Mel..." Riley sits with her hands on the wheel but doesn't turn the car on. "Are you sure?"

"You know, I've been thinking about this over and over for the last few days. It was so hard to decide because I was afraid of getting hurt by him again. I thought I could put the past behind me but I realize now I can't, because clearly he can't either. There's a reason we didn't work out back then, and it's the same reason we couldn't work now."

"What if you're wrong?"

I text Jamie that I left his key under his mat and turn my phone off.

"I might be but I'd rather be wrong than test it out only to discover I'm right and get hurt again. Please go."

Riley doesn't argue this time.

Chapter 17: 10 Things I Hate About You

"I'll be moving on Wednesday," Rose informs us after the Technology 101 for Seniors on Monday.

"Oh," I give her a sad smile, "it's so bittersweet. I'm so happy and excited for you but I'm going to miss you."

"Oh sweetheart," she hugs me, "just so you know, I've decided you're my honorary fourth grandchild so you can come visit me anytime you want."

"Don't say anytime or I'll take you up on that and start driving you crazy," I joke.

"I've been so blessed by your friendship that would be impossible," she pats my hand. "Where's Jamie?"

"Who cares," I mutter under my breath.

"Excuse me?"

"A few things have happened since I saw you last...."

"Do tell," she sits down next to me.

I tell her about breaking up with Sebastian and him snapping and about sleeping with Jamie and him saving me. Then about seeing him with Nicole.

"Goodness, a few was an understatement," she rubs her cheek. "That's a lot for anyone to be dealing with. Are you okay?"

"Honestly? No. I'm completely overwhelmed and angry and frustrated and at a loss of what to do. About anything"

"I can only imagine," Rose gives my hand a comforting squeeze.

"I want to dig a hole in the ground and bury myself in it for a few days. Not talk to anybody or anyone."

"Why don't you take the week off and come with me to Chicago. All of my things are being taken by movers but I could use the company on the drive again."

Can I do that? I'm sure Grace would understand once I tell her what happened. I am still scared Sebastian could reappear. The added benefit of avoiding Jamie is too much to pass up.

"You know what, that sounds like just the thing I need. Thank you, Rose."

"Can I give you my two cents about Jamie first?"

"Ugh," I throw my head in my hands, "I guess."

"Talk to him. Maybe everything isn't quite as it seemed."

"You know what I realized when I saw Nicole? Some part of me will always be afraid of him hurting me and that's not fair to him. I know he's changed but I can't forget our history and I can't help but be certain I'll always be wondering when the day will come he'll get bored with me and leave me for Nicole or some other woman that's better, more attractive, and has way less baggage."

"Doesn't he deserve to hear all this?"

"Yes," I peer down at my hands in shame, "but I don't have it in me to do it yet."

When I turned my phone back on Sunday night, I had a handful of texts and calls from Jamie. I let them go unanswered. I knew it would turn into a fight and I have no more fight in me. Plus, I know he'll try to get me to change my mind and I don't want him to change my mind. I'm still getting a text here and there but I don't reply yet. Grace mentioned he'll be back at work tomorrow so I'll catch him in the parking lot before the day starts and get it over with.

I let Grace know the situation and that I'm not up to working this week and she doesn't seem pleased to be losing me for four days but understands where I'm coming from, especially since the police were in to get security footage. The day ends and I've spent my emotional energy but I want to stop at the store for a bottle of wine. I'm hopeful a tall glass will help me forget my problems for a few hours but I think it'll mostly just make my emotions intensify. My plan is to watch my favorite movies and sing terribly to songs that make me cry. I'll have to turn off my phone so I don't drunk text or call anyone stupidly.

Hours later, I'm sitting on the couch sappily repeating line by line the amazing poem Kat reads to Patrick Verona in *10 Things I Hate About You*. Talk about big feelings. What would my things I hate about Jamie be? In my loose inhibitions and drunken state, I grab a pen and paper and start writing.

I hate the way you appear,

everywhere I don't expect,

I hate the way you make me laugh

and make me catch my breath,

I hate the way you're always there,

forcing me to second guess,

I hate the way you make me feel,

I just have to confess,

I hate the way you always dress,

so confident and sure.

I hate the way each moment with you

is never quite a bore,

I hate the way I smile

when I listen to your soft snore

And I hate how much our time together

makes me want you more.
I hate the fact you think you know me,
and the annoying way you're right.
I hate how much I want you there
when I turn off the light.
I hate that you came back around
and changed all that I knew
I hate how much I know you care;
I didn't have a clue.
I hate that I have to make a choice;
I hate the time has come
To tell you that our time together is near to being done
I hate how much you want me
and that you make me want to fight,
For me, for you, for all that we could ever do,
until we say goodnight.
You see Jamie, I don't hate you,

but I hate that we could never be

Together, lost in love and blissfully, totally free.

As I underline the last word, the flood of tears bursts from me, and I lose it. I love the written word but I've never been good at writing. Strong feelings and alcohol allowed me to release everything I've pent up inside. It's crazy cathartic.

There's a knock at the door.

My stomach drops.

Am I put together enough to open that door?

"Mel, please open the door, I know you're in there."

"Fuck," I muter to myself.

"Hold on," I shout loud enough for him to hear me.

I run to the bathroom to make sure I don't look too much of a mess. Not that it matters anymore.

"Hi Jamie," I open the door and every ounce of conviction I have blows away with the fall leaves in the crisp evening wind.

God, he's so hot. Even with the cuts and bruises. Maybe especially with those.

I know it would be a bit of a mixed signal after all those missed calls and texts, but the temptation to rip his red shirt right in half and throw him on my bed is almost too strong to resist. His eyes would watch me with irresistible wanting and we'd fall into the sheets and-

"What the hell Mel?"

Right. Back to real life.

"I've been meaning to send you a text."

"After you left Saturday morning, I thought we were on the same page. Congratulations on keeping me on my toes."

"I just decided about us and wanted to tell you in person," I stare off into the distance.

"Why do I feel like it's not the same way you were leaning on Saturday? What the hell happened? When did you drop my car off? Why didn't you knock on the door"

"Right before I sent the text. I saw you had company and didn't want to bug you," I stare into his eyes now so he can see the feelings behind the words.

"I was afraid of that," he shakes his head.

"Afraid is an interesting choice of words," I can't help but bite back.

"God, nothing happened Mel," he throws up his hands before settling them on his hips.

"I know," I cross my arms.

"You do?" His eyes squint in confusion. "Then why the ice barrier?"

"Seeing you and her together, it made me realize you and I aren't meant to be together."

"What? But nothing happened! I don't understand what the hell is going on," he walks inside the apartment and shuts the door. "Were my feelings about us not clear? Nicole is really just a friend. I know that's a line that's probably hard for you to believe but I promise it's true."

"I'm sure you believe that," I place my hands on my hips and frown. "I just don't think I could ever feel confident enough in our relationship to make me believe that."

"God Mel, she's married with kids! She was in Cleveland on business and my mom posted on Facebook asking for thoughts and prayers for healing for me and she reached out in concern and came to check on me. That's it. I promise there's nothing going on between us."

"Okay," I throw my hands up by my shoulder, "and what about the day she's not happy with her husband. Is she going to come running back to you? What if someone else comes along that you like more? I can't lose you again. Not like that. So I think it's better not to risk it at all."

He walks over and cups my face with his hands and says, "Do you want me to kick her out of my life? Is that what you want?"

"No!" I pull myself away and turn so I don't have to face him. "I don't want that! I want to be able to be with you and not be constantly worrying I'm not good enough for you. I forgive you for what happened five years ago and I truly think nothing happened with Nicole on Sunday but I don't think I can toss aside those feelings of anxiety and heartbreak I've internalized for five years because we have a touch of feelings for each other again. It's not enough."

"You're wrong," he walks to my other side so we're facing each other again. "I don't have feelings for you Melody. I am in love with you. I have been for a long time. I just didn't realize it until recently. Please tell me what I can do to make you believe that not only are you good enough for me, but you're the most amazing woman and the only one I could ever want."

His words put my heart in a vice grip and I can't shake free. He loves me? Are his words true? Or are they just true *now*? It's easy enough to say these things at the moment but what about tomorrow? What about a year from now?

It's not enough.

"I'm sorry Jamie," I grab the poem from the coffee table and walk to the door, swinging it open in a huff. "Please go."

"Melody," his eyes are begging me not to shut the door, "don't do this."

"I'm doing what I have to do. What's best for both of us."

He stares at me for a few seconds before his shoulders sag in defeat and he storms out the door.

"Here, I want you to have this," I hand the poem to him before he gets too far from the entrance, "I hope it helps you understand."

He gives the page the briefest glance before shoving it in my pocket and walking away from me.

Probably forever.

My heart breaks in a way I didn't know it could.

Goodbye Jamie. Thank you for letting me have you again if only for a little while.

Chapter 18: Better Than Revenge

I feel like I'm existing in a parallel universe, floating by and watching as everyone else lives their lives. Nothing feels real. I was so sure of my decision to end things with Jamie before they started again and I knew it was going to hurt. But I thought knowing it would be better for both of us in the long run would help soften the blow. Yet, it feels like I tore a piece of my heart out and ripped it to shreds.

"Tell me how I can help you?" Riley rubs my back as I lay on the couch with my face shoved in a pillow.

"Tell me I made the right decision," I say with a muffled voice.

"I can't do that," Riley says. "And it wouldn't help if I did because you're the only one who knows if that's an accurate statement or not."

"Fine, then I don't want to talk about it. Talk about anything else."

I shove my face back in the pillow as she gushes about Jackson. At least one of us is having their fairytale.

"I'm so happy for you Riley," I sit up and hug her. "I love that this is happening for you."

"Thanks sweetie," she hugs me back.

"I just wish things were going better for you," she says, "this was supposed to be the start of new and wonderful things for you and so far it's mostly been bad luck."

"Tell me about it," I mutter.

"You'd tell me if you were starting to feel like..." she pauses, "you know, how you did back then."

"I think so," I put my hands under my head in the typical pose for sleep, "I feel really sad and anxious and there are moments where the things I'm thinking remind me of thoughts I had back then but it doesn't feel as hopeless. Yet."

"Remember that you've got me, Rose, and your family. You're okay. I know it hurts now but we'll get you through this."

"I want him," my voice breaks, "I want him so bad. What if I'm being stupid? What if I should have said fuck it and gave into my feelings?"

"It's a tricky thing deciding whether to let your heart or your head win. The best solution is a compromise. Let your heart guide you while your brain advises. Make decisions that feed your soul but take each step toward that decision with a conscious awareness of the important things like what will keep you safe."

"I'm not sure that made sense to me," I groan.

"Give it a couple more days," she laughs, "you're still in the thick of being miserable. Things will become clearer the more distance you have."

"Guess it's good I'm going to Chicago then," I sit up, "both literal and figurative distance is necessary."

"You're going to be okay," she squeezes my hand.

"At least one of us seems sure of that," I sigh.

Part of me hopes I'd look down and see a text or a call coming in from him. *Fight for me Jamie.* I want him to prove to me I'm wrong. He probably knows, even if it's deep down, that I'm right. There's no fighting fate.

The call never comes.

I knew I made the right choice.

Tuesday comes and goes and soon enough it's bright and early Wednesday morning and Rose and I are on our way. I briefly regale her with Jamie's visit but tell her I don't want to talk about it anymore than that.

The drive is so uneventful. Rose plays all of her favorite songs of the sixties and seventies and I love every minute. We sing to The Mamas & The Papas, The Supremes, Elvis, The Beatles, Marvin Gaye, and so many more. Such good music. I love a lot of modern music but it's so different from the oldies. It's a different kind of soul.

I let myself pretend everything that's happened in the last few days happened to somebody else. That I'm free from the heartbreak and pain and fear and only have happiness and fun to look forward to.

Rose is so incredibly amazing and strong. The bravery she showed even to reach out to Mateo, let alone reconnect with him after all these years and then decide to move three states away to be with him for the time they have left in this world. If she could do all that, the least I can do is not completely lose my mind over a stupid boy.

Mateo is gleefully waiting for us - well, Rose - on his front porch. The only smile I've seen bigger is on Rose's face when she sees him waiting. Now, that's love. It's beautiful.

Could Jamie and I have had that? The thought comes out of nowhere and I push it back down but not quick enough to avoid the searing pain of heartbreak. What's the point of anything? Nothing ever works out the way you want it to, so why even try? I tried to get back out there with Sebastian and look how that went. I got my "dream job" and it's led to all this. Just more hurt and confusion.

Stop it Melody. Don't start with that. It's a slippery slope to crossing the street without looking both ways. I'm so weak. So pathetic. I hate it. I want it all to stop. Can't I just stop caring so much? About every goddamn thing. It would be so much easier.

Focus Melody. You're here to help Rose and celebrate her joy. Not get all pathetic about your own issues. Nobody needs that.

Maybe nobody needs me. Rose has Mateo. Riley has Jackson. Jamie will make his way back to Nicole or somebody better than me. The only person who seems to need me is Sebastian, and he's not exactly the picture of good mental health. Whoopie. Maybe Sebastian and I are more of a match than I thought.

Text Riley, my inner voice tells me. *Don't do this to yourself.*

I will. Later. I don't want to bother her.

"Oh, look at him," Rose says. "How did I get so lucky?"

"You're not lucky. You're brave. You made the choice that would bring you happiness. To him. No luck involved."

"And what choice do you have to make to bring yourself happiness Miss Melody," Rose gives me a knowing expression and then hops out of the car like a sixteen-year-old in love before I have the chance to answer.

Good question Rose. At what point does happiness trump protecting myself?

I move all of Rose's bags and small boxes from the trunk and backseat to the garage. When Mateo and Rose finally stop kissing and embracing, they help too. The movers aren't supposed to arrive until tomorrow so the work is light today.

"Spend the day relaxing," Rose instructs me as she and Mateo show me the guest room. "You have nothing to do and right at this moment nothing to worry about. So don't."

"I brought several books and as long as I have access to a tea kettle I'm golden," I sit on the edge of the fluffy white bed.

"There's an electric kettle in the kitchen and a fully stocked cabinet of tea," Mateo tells me kindly.

"Forget I'm even here and go be a young couple in love," I tell them.

Rose and I hug before I push them out of the door. I fall back onto the bed with my arms splayed wide and simply lay there for a while. My brain shuts off. I stare at the ceiling and watch as the ceiling fan goes round and round and round and round. Then when my brain threatens to turn back on, I walk downstairs and make myself some tea. My instinct is to reach for the chamomile but that scent immediately brings me back to my last night with Jamie so I pick an Earl Grey instead. Bland like my soul. Ugh.

It's been too long since I've been able to lose myself in a book. I didn't realize how badly I needed to be somebody else. Somebody who can fight dragons and win. Someone who can explore mystical worlds and see beautiful and fantastical things. Why am I certain it would be easier to fight a literal demon than the ones hiding in the deep dark recesses of my soul? I wish I was in a place where I can wield a sword rather than the power of positive thinking.

The weekdays pass and I split my time between reading and helping Rose unpack. By Friday night, I feel a little more at peace with myself. I haven't thought about Jamie very much but the sadness lurks, ready to pounce at the first sign of letting reality back in.

After a dinner of Rose's famous beef stroganoff, we sit in the living room sipping wine in front of their fireplace.

"Talk to me Melody," Rose prompts, "lighten your mental load."

"I'm afraid to," I admit. "For a few moments I feel like I know how I feel and then I don't. I rethink it and second guess my decisions and it feels like an endless loop of questioning and uncertainty. I don't feel like I can trust myself or my choices."

"Why is that?"

"I don't know, maybe because what it is I want, what is best for me, and what I should do are three different things."

"Should do according to who?"

"I don't know. According to me? Me from five years ago would absolutely agree with the choice I made, but me now is clearly not as happy as I hoped I would be. As I want to be. Despite knowing everything I should do, the only thing I keep coming back to is that I miss Jamie. But seeing him with Nicole, even though I know nothing happened. It killed me. It brought me back to who I was five years ago and the parts of me that are vulnerable are clinging to the past so I don't forget what happened. So I won't repeat it."

"What would help you move on from the past? You know how Jamie feels. You know how you feel. Everything that happened back then wasn't just between you and Jamie. There was a third person involved. Maybe you need to talk with her too."

"Nicole? I don't think I've ever actually spoken to her."

"Maybe you should. Get some closure."

That would be awkward. But would it be helpful? Maybe. It could be worth a shot.

"Thank you, Rose."

"Anything to help the woman who helped reunite me with my Mateo."

It didn't take long to find Nicole on Facebook. I kept my brain turned off and sent her a message asking if we could meet up the next morning. She agreed and now I'm sitting in a Starbucks in downtown Chicago waiting for her.

The force driving my leg to tap tap tap over and over is not in my control. I don't know why I'm so nervous. I've spent so long convinced Nicole is the villain in my story and talking to her may do nothing but cement that feeling for me.

She walks in and starts surveying the room so I wave to her. As she gets closer, I realize she does look a little different than she did back then. More mature, with an air of confidence. Though I think the confidence has always been there.

"Hi Nicole, thanks for meeting me," I stand awkwardly when she gets to the table.

We're not friends so there's no hugging and shaking hands is too formal so I do a half wave and then gesture to her chair and she sits.

"Yeah, it definitely surprised me to get your message but I'm kind of glad."

"You were?"

"Yeah. It's a little funny we've had this connection but never actually talked."

"Well, we only had Jamie in common and it wasn't exactly a connection I wanted to continue to be there," I say with a little too much harshness.

"Right," she examines her hands. "Let me go grab a coffee and then we can talk."

"Of course," I watch her walk away and then rub my legs.

Come on Mel. Don't be such a bitch. You're the one that asked her to meet you.

"I do appreciate you meeting me," I tell her when she's back and I hope that shows I feel bad about before.

"It wasn't a problem. Can I ask why you wanted to meet me?"

"You know, that's a good question. One I'm not sure I have a good enough answer for," I sigh. "I'm going to be completely honest with you. I think maybe Jamie mentioned we work at the library now and have been spending a lot of time together. Which has led to us talking about getting back together again but I told him no. It was a tough choice, but I thought it would be best for both of us. The problem is I can't seem to move on from it. The choice I made stemmed from everything that happened five years ago and that involved you so I guess I wanted to get back to the root of it and see if it can help clear things up for me."

"I see," she casts her eyes down. "Jamie and I haven't talked too much over the last few years but we've been in each other's lives so long we always end up keeping in touch. Let me just say I'm sorry for everything that happened then. I'm not proud of it."

The question that I've been wanting to ask bubbles up to my lips and I finally speak it.

"Why couldn't you let him go?"

"Jamie was, and probably still is, one of my best friends. He was always there for me when I needed him, even when we weren't dating. That's rare to have and hard to lose. I became dependent on having him around. Jamie has such a good heart and he could never say no to helping someone he loves. And let's just say I needed a lot of help back then. I think we both became codependent like a rubber band. We'd try to separate and do okay apart for a little while but we always snapped back to each other."

"It's amazing how much he cares about other people. I saw it back then too. I think that's why it hurt so bad when he broke up with me and I knew it was because of you. Why did he care so much about you and so little about me?"

"Because I didn't let him," she admitted with her head down in shame. "Every time he took a step away from me I found a way to pull him back. I'm sorry I wasn't strong enough to let him go."

"I hated you for so long. Blamed you for what happened between me and Jamie but he made his choices. We all do. That doesn't make you a bad person."

"I've changed so much since then," she takes a sip of her coffee. "Jamie and I broke things off for good about a year after that. I met my husband Finn pretty soon after. Jamie and I were - are - best friends, but I realized pretty quickly that's all we should be. He did too. I think he was tired of not being confident about what we were to each other."

"And you don't think..." I pause feeling ashamed to ask, "you don't think you'll ever bounce back to him again?"

"No," she smiles and rests her hand on top of mine, "the easiest thing to say is I love my husband more than anything in the world and there's no reality where I leave him. But I promise that even if my husband wasn't in the picture, Jamie and I are through being together in that way."

"Okay," I nod and give her a smile of appreciation. "Thank you for understanding and talking to me about this."

"You know, Jamie mentioned your situation when I was visiting him the other day," she pats my hand and sips her coffee, "I've got to tell you, he never talked about me the way he talks about you. Jamie and I were a comfortable convenience. Jamie and you seem to be...inevitable."

"That's funny. That's what I always thought about you and him. You really think that?"

"I do."

"Thanks. This helped me a lot."

"I'm glad. I hope we can be friends now."

"Me too."

We finish our drinks and talk about her kids and I tell her about Rose and Mateo. When we part ways, I'm grateful for taking the chance to reach out to her. I didn't know what to expect or what I wanted to get out of it but I realize now it was clarity. I saw her as my enemy when I needed to see her as a person. Now I see her as a friend.

And Jamie...Jamie I see differently too. I thought his choices in the past were made with indifference to me but I realize now they were made with his best intentions for taking care of himself and Nicole, who he had known for much longer. That doesn't make them right, but it also doesn't define him as a person or who he is now.

I think deep down I've known this to be true, but I've been so scared of getting hurt again, I've been clinging to false assumptions for the sake of making a straightforward choice. It was definitely painful but in the face of fighting for us to be together; it was the easier choice. Fighting for love is one of the hardest and scariest things humans do. But it's time for me to be brave. It's time for me to fight for my happiness. For Jamie.

Chapter 19: Poems and Passion

"I'm going to miss you so much Rose," I hug her in front of O'Hare airport late Sunday afternoon. "It's been such a joy being friends with you."

"Distance doesn't take away from love, it adds to it," Rose responds. "It's a simple drive and Mateo and I have so many plans to travel. Lorain is my home and I'm sure it'll often be a stop along the way."

"Good luck," I hug Mateo too. "With everything. You two deserve every amazing thing you could want."

"So do you," Rose tells me before she and Mateo wave me off.

I've always loved airports. Airports are an in-between place. There's something exciting about how chaotic it is. People rush here and there to make their flights while others seem glued to their seats as they wait for their layovers. My favorites are the people who sit in the weirdest spots to gain access to an outlet to charge their phone or tablet.

I reach my gate and plug my headphones in and try to make a game plan for how I'm going to win Jamie back. Maybe it'll be as easy as telling him I love him. But I hurt him this time and I'm afraid it won't be so easy. I could show up at his apartment and confess my feelings on his doorstep. I'm so nervous about his reaction I'm not sure I'm courageous enough to do it tonight. Doing it at work feels wrong. Telling someone such a big, emotional thing in a public place is kind of rude.

Maybe it's not something I should plan. A declaration of love feels more like a spur-of-the-moment kind of thing bursting from true, enormous feelings that can't be contained at the sight of that person.

My brain is still going over and over the possibilities by the time my flight takes off and throughout the air. There was a slight reprieve as I marveled over the giant cotton candy clouds and breathtaking view. It's mind-boggling it's even possible for me to be flying in the air in a big metal tin fourteen thousand feet and higher above the ground. As I survey the Earth down below, it puts into perspective how small I am in the grand scheme of the universe.

Riley picks me up from the airport and I tell her about what I've realized and the choice I've made.

"That's so exciting," she squeals, "of course I didn't want you to get hurt but every part of me was screaming that you and Jamie are meant to be together."

"Meant to be together is unrealistic don't you think?" I chuckle.

"No, because I don't mean it in a fates are aligned, and the stars foretold your destiny sort of way. I mean it in a you two clearly love each other and if you love each other than you should be together kind of way. Obviously, it doesn't always work out, but I just knew it could with you two."

"I do love him," and I put my hand over my mouth in surprise, "I haven't actually said that out loud yet. To him – ever. Oh, my god. What if I can't do this? What if he changed his mind? What if me rejecting him made him realize it really was a mistake in the first place?"

My breathing gets heavier as I begin to panic spiral.

"Hey, hey, hey," Riley punches me in the arm hard enough to snap me out of it but easy enough to not do any damage. "Take a breath. That will not happen. Remember what I said about you being meant to be? Pull yourself together."

"You're right. I know you're right. I'm just so scared."

"I know, sweetie. It's going to be amazing. I know it."

"I hope you're right."

There's a lot of traffic for a Sunday night as we drive home from the Cleveland airport. I wonder if there was a big event in the city. I make Riley go the long way and we take Route 6. It runs right along the edge of Lake Erie for miles and miles and it's gorgeous. Especially now.

As we drive west, the sun dips lower in the sky. My favorite time of day begins, and hues of translucent yellows illuminate the world. During the golden hour, the world is dreamy and for a short period, it feels as though time has slowed and every move we make is touched by magic. Then, the sky transforms from striking gold to mixes of pinks, oranges, and purples. It's a kaleidoscope of color most artists could only wish to replicate perfectly.

"Can you stop at Lakeview Park?" I ask Riley a few minutes out from there.

"I promised Jackson I'd meet him at my place at seven, I don't want to be late," she responds.

"Just drop me off then. I'll get an Uber home."

"Or maybe call Jamie to come meet you," she winks at me.

"Maybe," I laugh.

She pulls into the park and lets me out with a, "love you Mel," and a side hug.

I find the bench with the best view and take a seat so I can admire the show the universe is putting on for what feels like only for me.

"Mel?"

At first I wonder if it's my imagination. Or maybe I conjured him here. Really though, I should have known. He always appears when I least expect but when I need him the most.

I turn to glance over the back of the bench and he's there.

"Jamie, what are you doing here?"

"I knew you were getting home tonight, and I was coming to talk to you but I got nervous about seeing you so I stopped here to think some more about what I was going to say. What are you doing here?"

"I wanted to watch the sunset. It was beautiful and I couldn't help but stop and admire it."

I stand and face him before asking, "why were you nervous?"

He starts a few times but never gets out a sentence. He moves and comes to stand beside me before gesturing for us both to sit. He plants himself at the far edge of the bench away from me. I understand why, so I make a move to be right next to him.

"Uh," he swallows nervously, "I'm not sure why I was nervous."

"What did you want to talk about?"

"I guess-" he gazes out at the lake before continuing, "I wanted to understand better why you said no."

"Right Jamie I-" I start but he cuts me off.

"Look Mel, I know we have a history and I know seeing me and Nicole together was probably not the best thing for my case but I will do anything to convince you nothing happened with her and that you should give us another chance."

"Jamie I-" I try again but he doesn't let me get a word in.

"I have spent the last few years, especially the last year, doing everything I can to be better than the guy you knew in college. I think I've been successful but maybe I'm wrong. Tell me what I need to do to be a man you could love."

He stands again, his emotions too big to stay sitting, "Melody, I think you're amazing and beautiful and kind and funny. And so goddamn sexy I can hardly contain myself when I'm around you. I love spending time with you and being around you makes me a better person so every minute apart is a minute I wish I was with you. I can see us having an amazing future together with so much fun and laughter and love. I know it won't be easy but I truly believe it'll be so unbelievably worth it."

"Jamie stop," I stand, completely at a loss from his words.

"Fuck," he shakes his head and searches the horizon, "I knew you'd still say no."

"Jamie, I spent the last twenty-four hours trying to think up the right words to say to you to convey how I feel and-"

"I know," he peers at the ground and takes a step further away, "you don't even have to say it."

I take a step toward him and grab both of his hands to make him face me, "you took the words right out of my mouth."

"Wait," he smiles so big, "I did?"

"Jamie, I made a mistake," I step even closer so our faces are only a breath away, "I made a decision based on fear instead of choosing what I really wanted. I'm sorry it took me so long but I know now what I really want is you. I'm not sure I could put it into words better than you but I feel the same way. I love you Jamie. I started falling in love with you five years ago, I've fallen so unbelievably in love with you now, and I hope in twenty years I'll be even more in love with you than ever. As much as being with you scares the ever living shit out of me, every ounce of my heart and soul is screaming you and I are meant to be together and no amount of logic or fear can overcome that. I love you Jamie. So much."

"I can't believe this is happening," his voice is little more than a whisper but he leans his forehead to rest on mine. "I love you Melody. I love you so much."

His body shifts and the next thing I know his arms are wrapped around my waist and he's lifting me and swinging me around while cheering and laughing out loud. His delight is contagious and I'm laughing too.

When he stops spinning around. His hands find the side of my head and his lips find mine. Every kiss Jamie and I have shared is magical and wonderful and I hope they continue forever.

"I wrote this for you," Jamie pulls a piece of paper from his pocket and hands it to me. "I didn't know how this was going to go and your poem inspired me I guess."

He shrugs as I reach for it and begin reading.

Melody: A Love Poem
By Jamie Washington

I love the way you smile;
it brings warmth to my heart

Rebekah Santoro

I love the way you do your hair,
to me it's a work of art
Your face is a vision,
your body drives me mad,
The thoughts they give me,
might be considered bad
I know these rhymes are not the best,
but listen to my words
Please know how much I mean them
even when I sound absurd
I've made a few mistakes
but I know you see the real me
It makes me believe in second chances;
it makes me feel free
I hate the way regret has been living in my mind
Losing you so long ago - God I was so blind
Because I love the way you help
and care about anyone you can
Falling head over heels in love with you
was never quite the plan
Yet your voice, your laugh, hell even your name
is music to my ears
Your amazing bravery inspires me

to face all my crazy fears
My wonderful Melody
you're so beautiful, kind, and strong
When we fight (and I know we will)
I can't wait for you to prove me wrong
You told me all the things you hate
about falling in love with me
I can only hope this short poem will help change your
mind and together we will be.

Tears spring to my eyes and I can't contain them. Is it the most beautiful poem in the world? Probably not. But to me, it's written proof that Jamie really loves me and he wants to be together, for better or worse. That he sees all of me for who I really am and wouldn't change a thing. I love him so goddamn much and I know the love Jamie and I share can conquer fear and doubt and is worth fighting for.

The sun continues to set and Jamie and I stay on the side of Lake Erie for a while, indulging in the elation that has come from our confessions of love. Soon, the sun has set and the warmth of home and our bodies being as close as we can make them is calling.

As we fall into my bed and make love in the awakening night, all I can think about is how happy I am. Months ago, I was sure a dream was coming true but then suddenly it was a nightmare.

Now, that nightmare has transformed back into more than a dream. Being with Jamie, my job at the library, my friends, my family- all of it is a beautiful reality I've worked hard to make happen, and that's better than any dream because there's no waking up from this. Each day I get to live a life full of happiness, love, and wonder and that's all I could possibly ask for.

Epilogue: Invisible Strings Tie Us All Together

Dear Rose,

I can't believe you and Mateo are in Indonesia! I've heard it's so beautiful. It's hard to imagine it's been eight months since I've seen you in person but I'm so overjoyed you and Mateo are traveling the world and enjoying your time together. When you get back to Chicago next month, Jamie and I will have to visit. I'm so glad I'm able to email you while you're half a world away. Those Technology for Seniors programs were an amazing thing for you for more than one reason.

Speaking of the library, I've been dying to tell you, I was accepted into a Master's in Library Science program and starting in the new year I'll be on my way to becoming a real librarian! My manager Grace has already promised me a librarian position at the library. I'm so excited. I've dreamed of being a librarian since I was a little girl. I'll have to work on my cardigan collection and my "shushing techniques."

Riley and Jackson are actually traveling right now too. They're doing a great American road trip. I'm pretty sure they're somewhere in Texas right now. Or Arizona. One of those two. I just made her promise she'd find a library in each state she visits and take a photo for me. Oh, and bring me a souvenir from her favorite place she visits. I'm pretty sure she and Jackson are well on their way to getting engaged. They're so unbelievably in love and he tried to ask casually for my opinion on engagement rings with a convoluted pun involving the *Lord of the Rings*. I'm so excited for the two of them.

I'm sure you're wondering about me and Jamie. There's not much gossip because we're amazing. There have been moments here and there when my anxieties and fears act up but he's been so patient and understanding and when it comes down to it, our love for each other conquers it. I hope one day maybe we'll get married, but for now, we're so happy being together I feel no need to rush.

Each moment is more exciting than the last and we have so much fun. We take little road trips here and there to explore the state. Last weekend we went to Hocking Hills State Park, and it was beautiful. We went camping. Well, can you really call it camping when you stay in a cabin with plumbing? Either way, it's beautiful there in the summer and I got so many excellent pictures. Who knew Ohio had such a beautiful natural spot? We're already making plans to go visit the other state parks so I can take more photos.

My photography is definitely getting better, and I have so much fun doing it. Jamie's my biggest fan unless I'm taking photos of him. But he's my favorite subject. From drinking his morning coffee to being hunched over the computer in his pajamas with messy hair, those photos are my favorite. I'm planning on keeping up with the hobby, maybe get to a point where I sell my photos at art fairs when I'm better at it.

Jamie and I had to testify in Sebastian's trial a few weeks ago. It was hard. I'd done everything I could to forget that night but it was all still there. Talking about it in front of him and all the people in the room was so difficult but Jamie helped me through it. He got sentenced to five years in jail so I won't have to worry about him for a while.

I miss you but I hope you're having the most amazing time. I hope you're taking pictures too because we'll have to have a whole slideshow viewing of everywhere you've been with popcorn and chocolate.

Rose, this is Jamie. I was sitting next to Mel as she was typing this email and figured I'd just say hi myself. I miss you too and hope you're having a great time. Also, when we visit you in Chicago, Mateo will have to make us his famous enchiladas again because I have had none as good since.

I've been meaning to thank you for calling me that day Mel flew home from seeing you and telling me to go talk to her. That life-changing moment will be preserved in my mind forever and it's all thanks to you. Telling Melody next to Lake Erie at sunset I love her only for her to tell me she feels the same was the best thing that ever happened to me and couldn't have been more perfect.

Stay safe and have an amazing time. We'll see you soon.

Okay, it's Mel again. I don't have much else to say so I'll leave this email with a thank you too. You're an inspiration and I feel so grateful to call you my friend. I have so many amazing people in my life and I'm blessed you're one of them. Talk to you soon.

Your honorary granddaughter,
Melody

Author's Note

Thank you to each and every person who has taken the time to read this book. From my early alpha and beta readers, my ARC readers, and now you, each set of eyes on this novel means the world to me.

If you enjoyed my book, please leave a review on Amazon, Goodreads, or other social media platforms. Reviews, good and bad, are what help indie authors like me get the word out and find new readers.

It's hard for me to believe I have one book published, let alone two. I hope to keep creating and keep sharing my words and my stories with everyone who will read them. "Regret & Romance" is a novel that has deep meaning for me and I sincerely hope people connect with it, enjoy it, and share it with others who might feel the same. I have loved romance novels for as long as I have loved reading and I can only hope my book does justice to the genre.

I want to especially thank my family and friends, without whom this book wouldn't be possible.

Thank you again,
Rebekah Santoro, Author